'There's definitely something not quite right!' Holly said. 'A millionaire doesn't just drop out. That doesn't make sense!'

Tracy's face lit up. 'Uh-oh, Belinda! Can you hear the Adams brain beginning to start up?' she teased. 'We'd better watch out!'

Belinda agreed. 'What are you thinking, Holly? What does your suspicious mind tell you *this* time?'

'I don't know. But no wonder the newspaper reporters are on Steffie's trail,' she said.

Tracy nodded. 'Do you think Steffie's deliberately lying?'

'Or is she just genuinely upset?' Belinda asked.

Holly shrugged. 'I'm not sure what's going on here. But I am sure of one thing.' She paused. 'This is something we should investigate, after all!'

The Mystery Club series

Deadly Games
The Mystery Club 9

Fiona Kelly

Hodder
Children's
Books

a division of Hodder Headline plc

Special thanks to Jenny Oldfield

Copyright © by Ben M. Baglio 1994
Created by Ben M. Baglio
London W6 0HE
First published in Great Britain in 1994 by Knight Books

10 9 8 7 6 5 4 3 2

A Catalogue record for this book is
available from the British Library

ISBN 0 340 60725 4

Typeset by Hewer Text Composition Services, Edinburgh
Printed and bound in Great Britain by
Cox & Wyman Ltd, Reading, Berkshire

Hodder Children's Books
a division of Hodder Headline plc
338 Euston Road
London NW1 3BH

1 A big break

Steffie Smith really was a pain! These days, she never printed an article in *Winformation*, the school magazine, without messing it up completely!

She was editor and her word was final. Ever since Holly Adams had arrived at the Winifred Bowen-Davies School, she had done her best to get on with Steffie. She knew a newcomer had to work her way in, and she desperately wanted to follow her ambition to become a journalist when she left school.

This time though, Steffie had gone too far! Holly scrunched up the latest copy of *Winformation* and marched down the corridor.

'Uh-oh!' Tracy said, peering out of her classroom. 'Holly looks real mad about something!' Tracy Foster was one third of the Mystery Club. Energetic and friendly, she was always ready to follow a mystery when it occurred. But Holly ignored her. She headed for the library and the *Winformation* desk there.

Tracy beckoned Belinda Hayes and they both set off in hot pursuit.

'Shh!' Belinda warned, looking over Tracy's shoulder. She was the other member of the Mystery Club. She lived life at a much slower pace than Tracy, but she loved mysteries every bit as much. 'I think it's something to do with the magazine!' she said.

They followed more cautiously now.

Holly was in no mood for fooling around. In fact, she'd hardly ever felt this cross about anything in her entire life. She swung open the library door and turned into the corner partitioned off for school magazine business. Sure enough, Steffie was there.

'Look at this!' Holly slammed her copy of *Winformation* down on Steffie's desk. It was open at the sports pages. She didn't even pause for breath. 'OK, so lately you've given me all the sports reporting! I've gone to all the first year soccer matches. I faithfully reported every deadly dull rounders ball ever thrown! I wrote virtually the entire sports pages single-handed. And what do you do? You miss out the scores! Look, not a single result printed! They were all in a neat little league table to show who was winning overall. And you left it out!' Holly felt her face grow hot with anger. Her grey eyes sparkled, her forefinger jabbed at the offending page.

Steffie glanced up. 'Have I? Oh, yes.' She looked down again at the piece she was working on, half-written in front of her.

2

'Is that all?' Holly stepped back amazed. She'd expected excuses, maybe even an apology. After all, it was the first time she'd ever complained to Steffie about anything.

'What? Oh, sorry,' Steffie said. 'Listen, I have to get on with this review. What's the name of Juliet's family in *Romeo and Juliet*, can you remember?'

Holly couldn't believe her ears. Steffie Smith was actually asking her for a piece of information! 'Capulet,' she said.

'Thanks,' Steffie said absent-mindedly. She jotted it down. 'Who played Romeo in the school production?'

By this time Holly was wide-eyed, but her brain was racing. 'Tom Benson. Uh, Steffie, you look as if you're under a bit of pressure here.' She leaned both hands on the edge of Steffie's cluttered desk. There were bits of paper, floppy disks and books everywhere. Holly's natural desire to help out someone in trouble was winning through. Anyway, she caught scent of an interesting problem behind Steffie's odd behaviour. 'Do you need any help?' she asked.

'Maybe,' Steffie sighed.

'Well,' Holly said, trying to keep her voice calm, 'why don't you let me write that review? I'd be glad to finish it off for you.' What she really meant was, 'I'd kill to do the arts pages; the play reviews, the films, the mystery books!' Until now, Steffie

3

had hogged them all and usually sent Holly off to freezing touch-lines and windy netball courts. Holly braced herself for the usual bossy Steffie Smith knockback.

'OK,' Steffie said quietly. She handed over the scrappy paper with its few scrawls. 'Two hundred and fifty words for Wednesday, please.'

Holly grabbed it. 'Thanks!' She thought at top speed and decided she would push her luck just little bit further. 'And I was wondering about something else . . .'

'Yes?' Steffie had turned to the empty computer screen and was staring blankly at it.

'Well, would you let me have a go at a couple of mystery pages for the next issue? You know, reviews of some good mystery books, reports on real life mysteries. That sort of thing. "Twenty things you should know about mystery writers"!' Holly ran through her ideas. 'What do you think?'

'Mystery pages?' Steffie frowned. Then she shrugged. 'Yeah, why not? Go ahead, do what you want.' And she turned back to the empty screen. 'But I'll need it for Wednesday so I can put it in the next issue.'

'I can let you have it by tomorrow!' Holly promised, before Steffie could change her mind!

She could not believe her luck – what on earth was wrong with Steffie?

*   *   *

4

'What's wrong with Steffie?' Tracy asked.

They were eating lunch in the dining-hall, sharing the packet of chocolate chip cookies Belinda had brought for her lunch. Steffie was hunched in a corner, her nose in a book, but obviously not concentrating.

'Who knows?' Holly wasn't interested right then. 'All I know is that she's given me a double spread for mystery news in the next issue!' She beamed at her fellow Mystery Club members. 'Isn't that great?'

'No!' Tracy yelped. 'I mean yes, it's fantastic news!' She could never hide her surprise. Steffie glanced up in the direction of the noise.

'She didn't!' Belinda bit thoughtfully into her coorie. She pushed her wire-framed glasses up her nose. Unlike Tracy, Belinda wanted time to digest this unexpected piece of news. 'That's quite a mystery in itself,' she quipped. 'Why on earth would Steffie want to give up part of her precious magazine?'

'Well, she did! And she gave me the *Romeo and Juliet* Review!' Holly insisted.

Belinda gave a slow smile. 'Well done, Holly. You've been wanting a chance like that for ages!'

Holly nodded. 'I know!'

'Wow, there must be something really wrong!' Tracy said. 'I can't think what could make a girl like Steffie look so down. Maybe it's boyfriend trouble?' She shrugged and went over to talk to Miss Baron, the music teacher, about violin practice, while Belinda still studied the lone figure in the corner.

Holly began to scribble notes for the *Romeo and Juliet* review; 'inventive production . . . talented actors . . . colourful costumes', when suddenly Belinda broke in with, 'No, it doesn't look like boyfriend trouble to me!'

'What?' Holly broke off. 'Oh, you're still going on about Steffie? Listen, as long as she doesn't change her mind about the mystery pages, I'm happy!'

But Belinda kept up the jokey investigation of Steffie's problems. 'From what I hear, Steffie's given up boyfriends to concentrate on her career! She eats, sleeps and lives for *Winformation*. That's what's so peculiar about her handing everything over to you!'

'Thanks a lot!' Holly stood up, pretending to be offended. 'I really appreciate that vote of confidence!' The bell had gone for afternoon registration and Holly started to pack her bag.

'No, I didn't mean that, Holly. I'm just saying how dedicated she is. It's not boyfriend trouble with Steffie. I'd say it was family problems!'

Holly glanced at scruffy, easy-going Belinda. Even in her school uniform, she managed to look like a bag-lady! 'Family problems?' she repeated.

'Yeah, they make you awfully moody,' Belinda

insisted. 'Moody and unpredictable, like Steffie is now. I'm telling you, that girl definitely has family problems!'

Holly raised her eyebrows. Belinda and Tracy could think what they liked. She made her way out of the crowded hall, giving Steffie an uneasy little wave as she went. As long as the all-powerful editor of *Winformation* didn't change her mind before the Wednesday deadline, Holly was happy!

The three girls met up after school as usual.

Ever since Holly had put the advert in the school magazine for fellow mystery book fans, she and Tracy and Belinda had become the best of friends. It had made the move up from Highgate to Holly's new home in Yorkshire so much easier. Even leaving behind her best friends, Peter Hamilton and Miranda Hunt, had seemed less painful because of them.

'Well, since we've no actual mystery on our hands at the moment, what do you two say to going into town for an ice-cream?' Tracy suggested. Ice-cream was one of the things the Mystery Club liked best. 'In the park, the ice-cream parlour, or the van in the carpark?'

'The carpark!' Belinda cried. 'It's nearest, and I'm starving!'

Holly and Tracy laughed. Belinda was *always*

starving. And they went straight down the hill into town to buy their favourite treat.

'I can't stop long,' Holly told them as they perched, ice-creams in hand, on a low wall by the flower beds. 'I've got to work fast on Wednesday's deadlines!' Phrases for her articles kept popping into her head, and she wanted to write them down before she forgot them.

'Hey!' Tracy said softly. 'Don't look now, but here comes your beloved editor. I wonder what she's up to?'

They looked over to where Tracy was pointing. Across the carpark by an expensive little boutique, they spotted Steffie Smith herself. She still looked miserable. They watched as she checked up and down the street and looked anxiously at her watch. Then, up drove the shiniest, smoothest looking sports car Holly had ever seen. It was a red convertible, with silver wire-wheel trims. The driver pulled up beside Steffie and stepped out.

'Can this be real?' Tracy gasped.

The driver looked as if he'd stepped out of a Hollywood movie. He was about twenty years old, with a fabulous haircut. He was tall and handsome. His clothes were casual, but clearly expensive.

Steffie greeted him with a tiny peck on the cheek. He put one arm round her shoulder. She turned her face away and stood clear of him. He leaned against the car, apparently trying to explain something to

8

her. Steffie shook her head. She spread her palms, arguing, telling him something he didn't want to hear. He put his hands in his pockets, looking stubborn. He shook his head back at her.

'They're having a row!' Belinda breathed.

'Why would anyone row with someone that good-looking?' Tracy said.

'Shh!' Holly warned. If there were any clues, they didn't want to miss them.

Steffie had stopped arguing. She hung her head, and the two of them stood in silence, unaware of the envious stares of passers-by at the dream car. Then Steffie began again, talking at him, tugging at his sleeve. *No*, he was saying; *no*! Steffie turned away, said one last thing over her shoulder before she walked off. She walked away.

Tracy and Holly stared after the disappearing figure. Steffie went down the street, cutting through the Victorian arcade. And she wasn't coming back.

Belinda looked thoughtfully at the young man as he climbed back into his car. He revved the engine and slid off towards the main road in the opposite direction to Steffie. He didn't pause, and he didn't look back.

'See, what did I say? Boyfriend trouble!' Tracy declared triumphantly. 'Anyhow, I don't think it's anything the Mystery Club can get involved in.' She shrugged. 'Just a little argument, I guess.' She ate the last bit of her ice-cream and sighed. 'Who ever heard of a Mystery Club minus a mystery?'

'Yes, no need to write this down in the Mystery Club notebook!' Belinda sighed, then gave a little grin.

'I'm not so sure!' Holly said slowly. Was this just a simple boyfriend-girlfriend row? 'Shame,' she said, 'I was just getting ready for another good mystery!'

Belinda watched the red car disappear. 'Poor thing,' she said. She hated it when people argued.

'Who, Steffie?' Holly grabbed her schoolbag, ready to leave. For some reason she disagreed. Normally she would have a soft spot for anyone in trouble but she couldn't exactly bring herself to feel sorry for Steffie Smith!

Next day Steffie's temper had not improved!

She sat at her desk during lunch-break, shoving papers around. She snapped at a junior reporter and slammed a disk into the computer, ignoring Holly's approach.

'Did you see my review?' Holly asked as brightly as possible. She knew a lot rested on the success of the two pieces Steffie had agreed to let her do. She kept her fingers firmly crossed.

'Review? What review?' Steffie snapped.

'The *Romeo and Juliet* review you wanted. I put it on your desk first thing this morning!' Holly had been pleased with the piece. She'd shown it to Tracy and Belinda, and both had thought it was witty and to the point. She waited for Steffie's reaction.

'Oh, that review. I changed my mind, I want to do that myself after all.' Steffie didn't even bother to look round. 'I scrapped it, I'm afraid.'

'What!' Holly swallowed hard. *Keep calm*, she told herself. 'And what about the mystery pages?' She'd worked until midnight, getting together some snappy reviews of her favourite mystery books.

'Hmm, it's here somewhere, I think.' Steffie swivelled in her chair and began rifling aimlessly through piles of papers.

'Did you get a chance to read it?' Holly was hanging on to her patience, but only just.

'Not yet,' Steffie said carelessly, running one hand through her short blonde hair. 'I might have to hold off until the next issue.'

'What!' Holly felt she might explode. She watched Steffie failing to find the precious article. If it was lost, she'd do her editor some serious damage!

'Here it is!' Steffie exclaimed. She retrieved two crumpled pages from a drawer. 'Oh, no, that's something else.' She paused a moment and looked up at Holly with a vacant expression. 'It is Monday, isn't it?'

'No, it's Tuesday!' Holly couldn't believe this.

The normally efficient Steffie was in chaos! 'Tomorrow's the deadline for our next issue, remember?' She took a deep breath. 'And about this article on the mystery stories. You promised yesterday that it would be in this issue for sure!'

'Did I? Yes, you're probably right.' Steffie put a hand to her forehead. Then she gasped. 'Tuesday, you say? I haven't even started to write my editorial!' Her face was seized with panic. She turned on Holly. 'What are you doing standing there like a useless lump? You're distracting me from all these important deadlines!'

Holly froze. 'Now listen,' she said, controlling her voice as best she could.

'No, *you* listen, Holly Adams! You can't come in here trying to take over! Just because you did some little pieces of work on your last tatty little school rag, don't think you can march in here giving me orders!'

Steffie looked wild. She was pushing papers right and left off the desk. At one point Holly thought she was going to burst into tears. But she pulled herself together. 'I'm sorry,' she said, 'I shouldn't have said all that. Listen, Holly, I wonder if you've got a copy of that mystery stuff? I think I can find room for it after all.'

But Holly had been pushed too far. Mystery pages, or no mystery pages, she wasn't going to take any more of this!

She ignored the panic on Steffie's face. 'I'm sorry you see me as a useless lump,' she said. 'And I'm sorry you thought my work for my last magazine was silly. But as for going and fetching a copy of the mystery article which you've lost, I'm afraid you'll have to find some other way of filling the space!'

She turned, preparing to leave with a tiny scrap of dignity intact. Inside, she was ready to burst into tears, but she wouldn't let Steffie Smith see that.

'Holly, wait!' Steffie pleaded.

Holly ignored her. She paused just one more second. 'Steffie, you got yourself into this mess, and now you'll have to get yourself out! Don't expect any help from me!'

And she flung open the library doors. Holly marched out into the corridor with hot tears stinging her eyes.

2 Drop-out

'This is not normal. There's something Steffie's not telling anyone!' Tracy insisted. She was uneasy when things didn't quite add up, and Steffie's wild behaviour was puzzling. Besides, she didn't like to see Holly hurt like this.

She and Holly were making their way up to Belinda's house next morning, before they all set off for school together. 'Yes, it's odd,' Holly agreed. 'But it's not anything we can figure out for her. It's Steffie's business, not ours, isn't it?' She still doubted that Steffie Smith's bad mood could have anything to do with the Mystery Club. In any case, she was still upset.

'Hi, Mr Hayes!' Tracy called. 'Is Belinda ready?'

He was on his way from the house to the garage. 'You must be joking!' he said. He folded his newspaper under his arm. Mr Hayes was a wealthy businessman, always busy, always on time. Holly smiled at the difference between him and his easy-going daughter. 'When was she ever ready?' he sighed. 'Listen, she tells me there's a

14

plan for you three to get together at Holly's house this weekend, is that right?'

Holly nodded. 'It's Mum and Dad's wedding anniversary. They're going away for a couple of days and they said I can invite Tracy and Belinda to spend the night.'

'Hmm,' Mr Hayes grunted. 'Be sure you know what you're letting yourself in for!' he joked.

Holly and Tracy grinned. 'Anyway, here she comes!' Holly said.

Belinda sauntered out from the stable of her much-loved chestnut thoroughbred, Meltdown. Her school uniform was covered in scraps of hay.

'How long will you be?' Holly shouted.

'A couple of minutes!' She gave her father a goodbye peck on the cheek while Holly and Tracy went over to the stable. They treated Meltdown to some of the contents of their lunch boxes. Holly stroked his soft, velvety nose.

But Belinda seemed to have stopped in her tracks. She was still out on the drive, tilting her head sideways and trying to sneak a look at her father's newspaper. 'Just a minute!' she cried, seizing it from him.

'Belinda, I'm in a hurry!' he protested. 'I have an important meeting at nine-thirty.'

'We're in a hurry, too. School, remember?' Holly grumbled. But she did go over to see what was so exciting about the business section of Mr Hayes's

newspaper. 'Midas Man Drops Out' said the headline. 'What's wrong? Why all the fuss?' Holly
asked.

Belinda was speechless. She pointed to the
headline and the picture underneath. 'Head of
Starware calls it a day,' Holly read, though the
paper trembled in Belinda's hands. 'What's so
fascinating about this?'

'Belinda!' Mr Hayes repeated, impatiently swinging his car keys. 'Would you please give me back
my newspaper!'

'But look!' Belinda said at last. She pointed to a
picture of a man with a briefcase getting out of a
large limousine. 'Don't you see who it is?'

Holly studied the grainy photograph. 'It's Steffie's
boyfriend!' she said, astonished. There he was; tall,
fair-haired, in an expensive business suit.

'What did I say?' Tracy cried triumphantly.
'When we saw them in town yesterday, didn't I
say it was boyfriend trouble?'

But Holly read on: '"One of the youngest rising
stars of the computer world, twenty-two year old
Greg Smith of Starware Ltd., yesterday shocked
the business world by announcing his retirement.
He has built the software company into a million-
pound business. Everything he touched seemed
to turn to gold. But the stress of success has
beaten him. Yesterday Greg was unavailable for
comment."'

'See, it's the same guy!' Tracy was too excited at being proved right to pay attention to details.

'It's the same man all right,' Belinda said slowly.

'That's right; Greg Smith, youngest millionaire in a young man's world, computer software,' Mr Hayes said, rescuing his newspaper. He confirmed the story. 'A local family, as it happens. He's the success story of the year, and he gives it all up! I don't get it!' He went on his way to the garage, shaking his head.

'But . . .' Holly raised her hand to speak. He was already in the car and starting the engine. She turned to her two friends. 'You realise he can't be Steffie's boyfriend after all!'

'Why not?' Tracy said stubbornly. 'Why can't he be her boyfriend? Look, if he's decided to give up his business, it sure would explain the argument in the carpark, as well as Steffie's foul moods.'

'He can't be her boyfriend because he's called Greg Smith! Smith! That's Steffie's name too!'

Belinda nodded. Tracy looked taken aback. 'It's a common name,' she protested weakly. 'Maybe it's a coincidence?'

Holly shook her head. 'No, but if he's not her boyfriend, who is he?'

Mr Hayes's champagne-coloured car purred slowly past. He stuck his head out of the window. 'Her brother, I think. Fancy you supersleuths not knowing that. Ask your mother; she'll know!' he told

17

Belinda and gave them all a final wave. 'And don't be late for school!'

'Her brother!' Tracy repeated, open mouthed.

'Talk about missing the obvious,' Holly groaned.

Belinda cracked a wide grin. 'Of course, Steffie's brother! Didn't I say it was family problems?'

For the first time in the history of the Mystery Club, Belinda was the first to move. She ran inside, calling for her mother. Tracy and Holly were hot on her heels.

Mrs Hayes refused to offer the girls a word of information on Greg Smith until Belinda was standing ready, complete with lunch and schoolbag, on the front doorstep.

'Well?' Belinda insisted. She was trying her best to look ready. 'Tell us all about Greg Smith!'

Mrs Hayes picked a stray hayseed off Belinda's sweater. Her own clothes were neat, bright and expensive as usual. Her face was carefully made up. She sighed at her untidy daughter. 'I don't know "all" about him, as you seem to think. What I do know is that he is a very rich young man. Of course, they do have their problems.'

'Who, the Smiths?' Belinda winked at Holly. She could rely on the accuracy of her mother's gossip.

'Well, there's been a divorce quite recently. I knew the mother, Margaret Smith, quite well through the squash club. Her marriage was never

18

a very happy one. I think she felt that running butchers' shops wasn't quite the thing, that in some way she'd married beneath her. I don't know really.'

Mrs Hayes paused, then went on. 'Well, since the children were almost grown-up, she decided on divorce. Paul, the husband, was very cut up about it. He sold his shop here in Willow Dale and got some work out in the Middle East supplying food to a petroleum company. Margaret was desperate to get away from Willow Dale too, but Steffie said she wanted to finish school. So there was an arrangement; Steffie would stay with her brother, Greg, until she'd done her exams. It all seemed to be fine, as far as I could make out.' Mrs Hayes rushed through the story, one eye on the clock.

'But now Greg's dropped out, he's upsetting everything!' Holly suggested. 'No wonder Steffie's been in a terrible mood lately.' Holly felt a sharp twinge of guilt for having been mean to her.

'Yes, and that's all I know!' Mrs Hayes insisted. 'And you three have fifteen minutes flat to get to school!' She began to close the door.

'Thanks, Mum!' Again Belinda was the first to move. Holly and Tracy chased down the drive after her along the well-worn path to the school gates.

'So, is that the end of the mystery?' Tracy asked,

quieter than usual. 'It's easy to see why Steffie isn't coping well right now.' She knew all about family break ups since her own parents' divorce.

'Looks like it,' Belinda said. 'It seems like a perfectly normal explanation for Steffie's little rendezvous in town. No romance, no suspicious circumstances.'

'Maybe, maybe not.' Holly couldn't help feeling there was something odd behind this morning's headline. 'Anyway, how do you both fancy lending a hand with *Winformation*? Today's the deadline and Steffie will never make it without some help!' Then she gave each of them a small nudge. 'Besides, if we help with the magazine, maybe we can still find out more!'

'If there is more,' Belinda said doubtfully. 'Honestly, Holly, don't you ever let go?'

'No!' Holly replied. 'And I take that as a compliment!'

'She's usually right – especially about mysteries,' Tracy reminded Belinda. 'So I guess we'd better say yes about helping Steffie to meet this deadline. OK?'

She whistled cheerfully as they entered school through the main doorway, under the imposing portrait of the school's founder, Winifred Bowen-Davies. The portrait had kicked off the Mystery Club's very first investigation. They were very fond of it and the secret clues it contained.

20

'Won't Steffie notice how much you've changed your tune?' Tracy asked.

Holly agreed; she might. 'In the circumstances, I'd better tell her that we're happy to try and help this time. She's in no position to refuse. You should see the chaos on her desk!'

Belinda and Tracy both nodded. 'OK, see you at break,' they said. They'd help get everything on disk and ready for printing; if Steffie would let them near her precious magazine, that was!

Holly was tact itself when they all met up in Steffie's corner of the library at break. 'Hi, is there anything we can do?' she asked casually. 'Any little bits of finishing off?'

Steffie told them she'd had two free lessons earlier that morning. 'I think I've managed to get things organised. I've found your mystery pages,' she added sheepishly. 'They're not bad.'

Holly felt herself blush with surprise and a tiny tinge of pride. This was the first time Steffie had ever said anything nice about her work.

Belinda and Tracy both gave her encouraging grins and then accepted orders from Steffie, who pointed to the word processor so that they could see her work up on screen. 'Actually, there are a couple of other little pieces that need typing in if you've got the time,' she told Holly. 'There's this one here about a geography department survey of the rock formations up at High Almscliff.' She handed her a piece of paper.

This was a different Steffie; quiet, calm, almost apologetic. Holly smiled and sat down at the keyboard. 'What fun; going up on to Almscliff to measure and take samples and all that stuff!' She began to type in the report.

Belinda groaned. 'Sheer torture, if you ask me. All that climbing!' High Almscliff was a massive semicircle of black rock outcrops some fifteen metres high, way out on the moor.

For a while they worked smoothly, while Steffie put finishing touches to her editorial.

'What's the subject this week?' Tracy asked Steffie in her chatty way. Steffie's column could cover almost anything from school rules to classroom decor.

'It's about the amount of homework we get,' Steffie said. She was still distant, in spite of Tracy's friendly approach. 'It's a topic most people have strong views on. Now, do you mind if we all just get on quietly?'

Holly gave Tracy a warning look. Steffie seemed calm, but she could blow up at any moment, the way things were right now. She wanted to keep on the right side of her.

As the bell rang for the end of break, Steffie looked up with a sigh of relief. 'I think we might make it, thanks to you three!'

Holly relaxed and stood up, smiling. 'We'll be back at lunch-time,' she promised, as Mrs Dodson, the librarian, called Steffie over to answer an outside phone call.

But lunch-time plunged them all back into chaos. Steffie's face was like thunder again. Her desk was a mess. Tracy and Belinda did their best to make themselves invisible as Holly picked up Steffie's editorial article and began to type it up. No one spoke.

It was Steffie who broke the silence. 'It's none of their business anyway!' she exploded. Holly felt she was close to tears. 'I can't have reporters ringing me up at school! They poke their noses into something completely private. It's just not fair!'

Holly nodded sympathetically, though she wasn't at all sure what was going on. 'Is this about your brother's decision to leave his company?' she asked carefully, trying to keep the balance between minding her own business and offering Steffie a chance to talk.

'Yes. What Greg decides is his own affair. It's a perfectly straightforward thing. He's not cut out for the rat race, that's all. He wants some peace and quiet so he's found a little, out-of-the-way place for a while. What's wrong with that?'

'Nothing,' Holly agreed.

Tracy was listening hard. 'You mean he's actually

23

disappeared?' When Steffie said 'a little, out-of-the-way place', what exactly did she mean?

Steffie hesitated, then nodded. 'Yes!' She glared at Tracy. 'So what?'

Belinda nudged Tracy with her elbow. 'I expect reporters can be a real nuisance to someone who likes his privacy,' she sympathised. She wanted Steffie to say more.

'Yes. Greg put out his statement yesterday afternoon, hoping they'd leave him alone once the papers had got hold of the story.' Steffie grunted with disgust. 'Some hope! They have the cheek to ring me and expect *me* to tell them where he is!' She furiously stacked papers and disks. 'As a matter of fact, I don't even know where he is!'

Holly glanced at Tracy and Belinda. That was difficult to believe; that Greg Smith would just vanish without telling his little sister where he was going.

'He didn't tell me for just this reason!' Steffie insisted. 'Because he knew everyone would hound me. He said, "It's better if you don't know for now." That's what it means to become a recluse, isn't it? Not to tell anyone where to find you!' Her voice was rising in an appeal to Holly; 'You can't be a recluse if you tell everyone your address, can you?'

'No,' Holly said carefully. She realised there was in fact a lot more behind this than Steffie was

24

saying. 'So yesterday afternoon was the last time you saw him?'

Steffie gave her a hostile stare. 'In town? Yes. After he'd put out his statement to the press.' But she'd clammed up. They wouldn't get any more information, it seemed.

'We just happened to be there in the carpark,' Holly explained. 'We thought you might be having a row about something.' Her voice had softened. She didn't want to pry, but she really didn't want Steffie to have to cope with these problems alone.

Steffie stiffened. 'Not at all. We were just saying goodbye. Greg wanted to explain everything to me in person.'

Holly exchanged glances with Belinda and Tracy as she recalled the scene; the shaking heads, Steffie storming off. That had been no ordinary goodbye.

'Listen, Holly,' Steffie said. She'd become cool and guarded. 'I don't want you joining in any of the gossip about my brother, OK?' She went over to look at the printer. 'In fact, I'd like to be by myself right now, if you don't mind. I can manage everything from here on!'

Holly took a deep breath. 'If you say so.' She joined Tracy and Belinda by the door. 'Look, Steffie, we know you must be really worried. We understand!' She wanted her to know the Mystery Club was on her side.

But Steffie tossed her head. 'Worried? What

about? Greg's dropped out, that's all. End of story!' And she turned her back, busy with the printer, determined to ignore Holly's sympathy.

'Wow!' Tracy said, out in the corridor. She dodged bags and knots of students all hanging around outside classrooms. 'End of story, I don't think!'

Belinda followed more slowly. 'I'm still trying to feel sorry for that girl; honest, I am,' she said. 'But it's not so easy.' She paused for further thought. 'Mind you, it must be tough to turn up to an empty house at night. And she's not exactly Miss Popularity when she's at school either!'

They stopped in the main entrance hall before they split up for afternoon lessons. The kindly face on the portrait of Winifred Bowen-Davies looked out at them.

'There's definitely something not quite right!' Holly said. School hummed with activity; students hurrying to lessons, teachers checking corridors, a delivery-man with a box of supplies. But Holly's mind was trained on Greg Smith's disappearance. 'A millionaire doesn't just drop out!' she said. 'That doesn't make sense!'

Tracy's face lit up. 'Uh-oh, Belinda! Can you hear the Adams brain beginning to start up?' she teased. 'We'd better watch out!'

Belinda agreed. 'What are you thinking, Holly? What does your suspicious mind tell you *this* time?'

'I don't know. But no wonder the newspaper reporters are on Steffie's trail,' she said.

Tracy nodded. 'Do you think Steffie's deliberately lying?'

'Or is she just genuinely upset?' Belinda asked. 'If my brother suddenly dropped out like that, I'd be pretty upset. If I had a brother!'

Holly smiled drily. 'Listen,' she said, 'if my darling little brother dropped out and disappeared, I'd celebrate!' Jamie Adams was like all younger brothers; an absolute nuisance.

Holly shrugged, smiled and got back to business. 'Anyway, I'm not sure what's going on here. But I am sure of one thing.' She paused. 'This is something we should investigate, after all!'

'Yeah!' Tracy agreed immediately. 'When do we start?'

'Oh, you're probably right.' Belinda sighed deeply. 'Oh boy, another mystery to solve! Just when I was hoping for a quiet life. You know; riding, watching the telly, eating!'

Holly grinned. 'You don't fool me, Belinda Hayes. You're as keen as we are to get moving on a new mystery!' She darted excited glances at the other two. 'Now, do you have any theories as to what we've got this time?'

'Kidnap?' Tracy murmured in an awed voice. She was immediately caught up in the most dramatic possibilities. 'Murder? I guess someone might want

27

to murder you if you're the youngest millionaire in the business! All sorts of people would be jealous!'

'Hang on,' Belinda said. 'I think we should check the evidence first.'

Another bell had gone. Lessons were about to start.

'I agree,' Holly said. 'Kidnap, murder or blackmail, who knows? But there's more to this than meets the eye.' She thought of this morning's newspaper account and Steffie's angry defence of her brother's decision to vanish without trace. 'Let's meet at the gates,' she said as the trio split up. 'This is definitely one for the Mystery Club!'

3 MOON MAZE

When is a mystery not a mystery? The question bugged Holly all through French and home economics.

Answer: when Steffie Smith denies there is one!

Holly sighed impatiently over the shortcrust pastry she was supposed to be making. No, that wasn't good enough! If Steffie denied there was anything wrong, that only made Holly more determined to get to the bottom of the problem. Usually, Holly attracted mysteries like a magnet. She wasn't used to having to dig for them. This, she thought as she slapped the pastry on to the board, was most frustrating!

'Careful, Holly,' Belinda cut in. 'This is a lesson in how to make pastry, remember; not a martial arts class!' She grinned and pointed at Holly's misshapen dough.

'What?' Holly began to pick sticky white lumps from her fingers.

'You're supposed to handle it lightly, not try to kill it!' Belinda pointed out. 'Anyway, watch out; here comes Miss Earnshaw!'

29

'Holly Adams, what do you think you're doing with that pastry?' the home economics teacher interrupted. She poked the sticky mess. 'Where's the flour to stop it sticking to the board?'

Holly felt herself go red and tried in vain to lift the pastry back into the bowl.

'Too late!' Miss Earnshaw sighed, looking down in disgust. 'Anyway, do something useful instead. You can take a message to the office for me!'

She made Holly scrap the pastry and wash her hands, ready to go on the errand. 'Ask the secretary if she can reserve two guest lunches for me tomorrow,' she said. 'Now, do you think you can manage that?'

Holly nodded. Belinda gave her a sympathetic grin as Holly fled from the room.

She half ran down the corridor, turned the corner into the entrance hall and almost bumped into a glamorous stranger!

'Sorry!' Holly gasped.

For a moment the woman seemed taken aback, as if Holly had stopped her from just slipping quietly into the building. But then she smiled. 'Think nothing of it,' she said in a low, smooth voice. 'Say, can you please tell me how to find the office?'

Holly nodded. She took in every detail of the woman's appearance. She was the sort you noticed, from the top of her flame-coloured hair to her shiny, stilettoed feet. She was in her mid-thirties. Her face and figure looked sculpted, her emerald-green suit was expensively tailored and her nails were manicured. She might have a job as a newsreader on TV, Holly decided. But what was she doing here?

'Are you a reporter?' Holly blurted out. She knew that the press were still pursuing news of Greg Smith. Maybe that would explain why this media-style person was visiting the school.

The woman smiled. 'Actually, no. Is this the way to the office?' She followed Holly down the corridor.

Holly nodded again. 'Here it is.' She knocked on the secretary's sliding glass panel and stood to one side, listening intently.

'Hi, I'm Susan Haigh,' the woman introduced herself. 'I work with Megaware International. I telephoned earlier today. We're aiming to set up links between our outfit and this school!' Her silky voice paused.

'Ah, yes!' The school secretary sounded impressed. 'Miss Haigh! You spoke to the Head, didn't you? Is she expecting to see you?'

'Well, not exactly. But since I'm in the area, I thought I could get this set up right away. I just happen to have a tiny gap in my schedule,' she explained. 'Tomorrow I'm in London. The day after, who knows where!'

'Just a moment please,' the secretary said. And she disappeared to confer with the headteacher.

'I'm fixing up work experience!' The woman tried to peer at the books and files on nearby shelves, but then she turned and smiled again at Holly. 'At Megaware we're keen on creating interest among young people!'

Holly smiled back. Why didn't she believe her? *I'm getting suspicious for no reason!* she told herself. *She's probably a very nice woman, genuinely interested in student welfare!*

'I hear you run a magazine here,' the woman continued. 'That could be a really good way to publicise our scheme. You know; we could advertise for people interested in joining us for work experience.' She looked intently at Holly. 'You wouldn't know where I could find the editor of the magazine, would you?'

'Right now?' Holly stammered. Something told her not to give anything away. She became more convinced that this woman was a reporter who was after a good scoop on Steffie and her disappearing brother. 'No, I'm sorry, I don't,' she said.

The end of lesson bell rang as they waited for the secretary to return. The corridors quickly filled with pupils moving from room to room. Holly noticed that the visitor looked sharply in every direction, then at her watch. When she wasn't smiling, her face was blank and expressionless, like a painted mask. Then she seemed to see something that interested her. Her green eyes widened. She caught her breath.

Holly looked round quickly. Back in the entrance hall kids were still milling about. Steffie Smith was there with one of her friends from the lower sixth. She glanced across to give Holly a wave. Then she froze. She'd seen Susan Haigh. Their eyes met.

Panic seemed to seize Steffie. She crumpled as if someone had punched her in the stomach, and she grabbed herself around the waist. She went white and closed her eyes. Holly thought she was going to faint.

She dashed across the hall to lend a hand. The crowds were melting away, back into their classrooms. 'Are you OK?' Holly said.

With an effort Steffie stood up straight. She pushed her fair hair back from her face. 'I'm fine, thanks. It's nothing,' she whispered, staring across the hall. 'Where did Sharon Hall go, do you know?'

'Sharon Hall?' Holly looked down the office corridor. The flame-haired visitor had vanished. 'No, I don't know. Listen, she told the office that her name was Susan Haigh!'

Still stunned, Steffie shook her head. 'No way! I'd know her anywhere. Her name's Sharon Hall!'

'Then why . . .? What . . .?' Holly's thoughts flew off in all directions. 'She told me some story

33

about work experience. I knew it sounded odd, especially when she asked me if I knew where you were!'

Steffie gasped.

'I didn't tell her, but then you appeared, large as life.' Holly considered Steffie's white face. 'This Sharon Hall – how do you know her?'

'I don't, not really.' Steffie sighed. 'She knew Greg, that's all. She was a girlfriend.'

'*Was* a girlfriend?' Holly echoed. She decided to confront Steffie with her theory. 'You mean, she's using her past friendship with Greg to get an inside story on his disappearance? She's a reporter, isn't she?'

Steffie gulped and nodded. She swayed slightly then stood upright again. 'Yes, she is. And she's the sort of woman who won't let anything get in her way, believe me. Hey, for the first time in my life I nearly fainted!' she said, trying to shrug it all off.

'You're sure you're OK?' Holly picked up Steffie's bag. 'Do you want me to take you to the sickroom?'

Again Steffie said no. 'I'm fine now, honestly!' But she was looking round every corner like a scared rabbit. 'Shouldn't you be in a lesson?' she asked Holly.

Holly gasped. 'Uh-oh!' She'd just remembered Miss Earnshaw's message. 'I'm in the middle of double home economics. Gotta go! See you later!'

she said with an apologetic laugh. At this rate she'd be put in detention for a week!

Sure enough, when Holly got back to her lesson, Miss Earnshaw gave her one of her special disapproving looks. 'Did you give my message to the office?' she checked. Then she kept Holly busy on small tasks while the rest of the group finished their baking.

'Tough!' Belinda commiserated in a whisper at the end of the double lesson. 'Listen, Holly, let's meet up in the library after school. We've got some serious thinking to do!'

Holly nodded. 'You don't need to tell me that!' she said. She'd save the latest news about their visitor-in-disguise until she met up with Tracy and Belinda in the library. As she wiped down the work surfaces, she wondered why the sight of Sharon Hall, alias Susan Haigh, had made Steffie feel faint. And why had she denied it? And why had Sharon Hall rushed off without seeing the Head? Holly wasn't sure of anything, but she couldn't wait to discuss it with her friends.

After school, the Mystery Club met up in the library as arranged. Holly and Tracy followed Belinda down to the newspaper racks, next to the mystery book shelves in the fiction section.

'We need to know more about Greg Smith!' Belinda declared. 'And the best way to find out is to look up the story in lots of different newspapers. We can check out all the known facts.'

'Great!' Tracy grinned. 'Hey, he's easily the best looking drop-out I ever saw!' she said as she pulled a newspaper from the rack and spread it on the table.

'Tracy!' Belinda and Holly sighed in unison.

'Well, here he is on the front page,' Tracy said. She took a closer look and began to scan the print.

'Let's see!' Holly said. She studied the handsome features of Steffie's brother and the headlines alongside: 'MOON MAZE MYSTERY!'

'Ready?' Belinda said. The three of them bent their heads together to read the article.

Before his bombshell decision to drop out and disappear, it said, Greg Smith had built up his million-pound business on the strength of one computer game. 'SPACE WALK outsold all its rivals. The blue and silver box is the best birthday present any kid could get!'

They read on. 'Greg Smith, the brains behind SPACE WALK, is only 22 years old. He wrote the programme on a portable computer during breaks from his day job as a trainee car salesman. He set up Starware Ltd. and within weeks SPACE WALK zoomed to number one in the computer game charts. It beat big rival Megaware International into a poor second place.

'Starware Ltd. also chose today to publicise

Greg's new game, MOON MAZE. "Even bigger! Even better!" spokesman Nick Powell claims. He played down reports that Starware's rival, Megaware, had tried to steal their brilliant new game. "MOON MAZE is safe with us," he said. "Watch out for it in the shops soon!"'

Holly read it once, twice. Belinda looked up at her face. Holly grabbed Tracy's arm. 'Read the name of that other firm again!' she gasped.

'Megaware International,' Tracy read out loud. 'Why?'

'Because I've just met a woman who said she works for them, that's why!'

'Where?' Tracy shook her head. 'I don't see what's going on!'

'Here! I saw her here in school this afternoon! I was about to tell you.' Holly was sure it was the same name, and no coincidence.

'What was she doing here?' Tracy asked.

'Lying!' Holly said. Her voice was firm and clear. 'She lied about her name for a start!' She hesitated. 'Then Steffie threw me off the trail.'

'Why? What happened?' Tracy looked up at Holly, her hand still poised over the name; Megaware International.

'Well, I was already pretty suspicious of her because of this big story breaking about Greg Smith. Then Steffie came by, spotted her and nearly fainted on the spot!'

'That doesn't sound like Steffie!' Tracy agreed.

'So you put two and two together?' Belinda prompted. 'What was she, some kind of reporter?'

'That's what I thought,' said Holly. 'I asked Steffie outright; was this woman a reporter on Greg's trail?'

'And?' Tracy and Belinda said together.

'Steffie told me yes.' Holly frowned.

'But?' Belinda went on doggedly.

'I think Steffie was lying too.'

'Oh help!' Tracy yelped. 'Everyone's lying! Can you please tell me what's *really* going on?'

Holly continued slowly. 'I'm not sure, but I think the woman was partly telling the truth. I think she does work for Megaware International. She's not a reporter after all.'

'She works for Greg's rival?' Belinda said thoughtfully.

'But what was she doing here?' Tracy asked.

'I think she was after Steffie!' Holly told them. 'But not to get an interview out of her. You know, I think it might be kidnap we're talking about, after all!'

The three friends stared at one another, poised over the MOON MAZE MYSTERY article.

'It says here that Megaware denies everything,' Belinda said. 'They say they never tried to steal the new game. Listen to this quote from their managing director; "We're in good shape. We don't need to steal anything!"'

'But it's strange that Greg Smith has vanished!' Tracy pointed out. 'The two things have happened together.'

Holly nodded. 'Maybe they *are* struggling to sell their own games and they kidnapped Greg to get hold of MOON MAZE,' she suggested. 'They certainly have the motive, with so much money to be made from it!'

They sat down to puzzle things out, elbows on the table. Greg Smith's handsome face stared up at them from the newspaper.

'But why would Steffie deny it?' Belinda said slowly. 'If her brother's been kidnapped, why would she cover it up?'

'Maybe she's in on it!' Tracy giggled.

'More likely she doesn't know!' Holly said.

Tracy's smile quickly turned back to a frown. 'According to her, Greg actually *planned* to drop out. That doesn't fit with our kidnap theory,' she pointed out.

'And another thing,' Belinda said gloomily. 'Why should they stop at kidnap? If there are millions of pounds involved and they want to steal his game, wouldn't they want him out of the way for good?' She paused. 'If we're right, that is.'

'Hang on, Belinda,' Holly said. 'Tracy's got a point; Steffie's actions are the real mystery here!'

39

Tracy nodded. Then she put up a hand and warned them to be quiet. Steffie Smith had just walked into the library! She was heading for the *Winformation* desk, but she looked down and saw Holly, Tracy and Belinda in a huddle over the 'MOON MAZE MYSTERY' headline.

'So!' she said in a loud voice that split the silence of the library, 'You three can never leave well enough alone! How come you're always poking your noses into other people's business?' She stood, hands on hips, all fired up again.

But then her expression changed. The colour drained from her face. Her gaze had switched from the Mystery Club to the glass window in the door behind them. Holly spun round to look. There, framed in the window, was the bright green jacket and wavy, shoulder-length, flame-coloured hair of Sharon Hall. Unmistakable, unflinching in her gaze, she stood there staring at Steffie. But when she saw Holly she gave a little flick of her hair and backed off.

'Come on!' Holly shouted. 'Let's go and find out what she really wants this time!'

As Sharon Hall began to back away, they dashed for the door. Holly wrenched the handle. The door was locked! 'Please use the upper library door' said a notice on the wall.

With a groan, Holly, Tracy and Belinda raced back up the stairs and out of the top door. They rounded the corner and charged down a flight of steps to where they'd last seen Sharon Hall. But she was gone.

'Which way?' Belinda gasped.

The corridors, lined with notice-boards, were empty. Around another corner a cleaner's polishing machine whirred.

'Down here!' Tracy yelled. She ran down the corridor. 'Did a woman come this way?' she shouted over the noise of the cleaner's machine.

The man shook his head. 'Not that I noticed.'

'Oh, you wouldn't have missed her!' Tracy said, before they backtracked down the corridor to the library.

'Let's try the main entrance,' Holly suggested. But she was beginning to lose hope. Sharon Hall was probably well away by now.

'She'd need an awful lot of cheek to use the main entrance if she is mixed up in a kidnap,' Belinda muttered, trying to keep up with Tracy and Holly.

'She has got a lot of cheek,' Holly confirmed. 'She's the sort who gives the impression that she's allowed to go anywhere, do anything.' They poured out of the grand main entrance, all three together.

'Look!' Tracy pointed up the drive beyond the beech trees. A figure in a green suit was just leaving the school grounds.

Again they sprinted, just in time to see Sharon Hall stepping elegantly into a mysterious, low, silver car, registration PC100. She swung her legs inside and closed the door.

Holly made a mental note of the number – easy enough – and got a good look at Sharon Hall's driver as he shoved the car into gear and executed a smooth U-turn in the road. He was unsmiling, leaning forward and swinging the steering wheel in rapid circles. Sharon Hall glanced back at the girls as the car sped downhill into town, but the driver kept his eyes on the road. He was wearing a white, open-necked shirt, his hair was short and neat, his complexion was dark. Holly tried to memorise it all; every clue, every last detail.

Tracy and Belinda looked at Holly and shrugged.

'OK, let's go talk to Steffie!' Holly decided. They marched back into school, determined to find out what was really going on.

Steffie was still in the library, leaning against her desk. She looked startled as the three girls walked back in. 'Has she gone?' she whispered.

Holly nodded. 'Who is she? What does she want?'

'I told you, she's a horrible reporter after a juicy story about Greg,' Steffie repeated, exasperated. 'I never liked her, even when Greg was going out with her.'

Holly sat down in Steffie's seat and fingered a

pile of papers on the desk. 'She's not a reporter. She told the secretary that she works for Megaware International,' she said slowly, watching Steffie's reaction.

The older girl flinched and tried a scornful laugh. 'She's lying. She's just a reporter after a good story!' she insisted. Her voice was high and hysterical.

'Oh, come on!' Tracy interrupted. 'You don't expect us to believe that! Why would you be so scared of some dumb journalist?'

Belinda caught hold of Tracy's arm. 'Hold on a minute, Tracy. Look, Steffie,' she said more gently, 'we only want to help. Why don't you tell us who this woman really is and why she's looking for you? What has she got to do with Greg's disappearance?'

Steffie rounded on her. 'I don't need your sympathy, Belinda Hayes!' she cried. She was in tears. 'I don't need anything from you three!'

Holly studied Steffie Smith long and hard. Steffie Smith; bossy and quick-tempered, but someone who was always in control. Someone you looked up to even if you didn't always like her. But here she was, crying and frightened, trying to pretend that everything was normal. 'You know more than you're telling us,' Holly said quietly. 'That's all I know.' She stood up face-to-face with Steffie.

For just one second there was a strange look in Steffie's eyes. It said, 'Please help me! I'm scared!

43

I don't know what to do!' But the look vanished. 'You're just guessing,' she said stiffly, and her eyes went blank.

Holly sighed. 'We've been reading about Starware and Greg's games,' she persisted. 'And the row he's been having with Megaware.' She noticed Steffie's back stiffen and the blank expression deepen. She'd stopped crying now. 'Look, Steffie, it's beginning to seem pretty strange, Greg giving everything up right at this moment. Are you sure he hasn't been kidnapped?' She'd come out with it straight. She stood and held her breath. You could never tell how Steffie would react.

But Steffie put on her most aloof stare. 'Kidnapped?' she repeated, full of scorn. 'Of course my brother hasn't been kidnapped! He's on a tiny island somewhere off the west coast of Scotland, that's all! He *chose* to go there. He doesn't want anyone to know. Got it?'

Holly nodded. She didn't break her gaze.

'That's all!' Steffie insisted again. 'No mystery for your beloved Mystery Club, Holly Adams! No kidnap! Now just leave me alone!'

4   Ghosted away

'It must run in the family,' Tracy said.

'What must?' Belinda took off her glasses and used the cuff of her sweater to wipe them. They'd just finished queuing for lunch next day.

'Wanting to be left alone!' Tracy said. She nudged Holly and pointed to Steffie's usual corner in the dining-hall.

Holly took a look at Steffie sitting all by herself, refusing to touch the plate of food in front of her. She seemed to be looking sideways around the crowded room to check that no one was noticing her.

Belinda put one hand to her forehead and looked tragic. 'I want to be alone!' she sighed, melodramatically.

Tracy laughed. 'I know you, you couldn't bear to be alone for longer than one hour!' she challenged.

'Who couldn't?'

'You couldn't, Belinda Hayes. Stick you on a desert island all alone for just one day, and your tongue wouldn't know what to do with itself. You just need people to talk to!'

Holly smiled. 'You can talk,' she told Tracy.

Holly glanced again at Steffie. 'We'd better pretend not to pay her any attention!' she warned.

They worked hard for the next few minutes at ignoring Steffie. Holly told them about the problem Mr Lupton, the technician, was having with the school printer. 'It's held up *Winformation* for a whole day this week. I hope we don't lose sales,' she said. Belinda and Tracy nodded seriously. But all the time Holly managed to keep one eye on Steffie's strange antics.

First, she poked at her meat pie and chips. Then she put her fork down. She covered the plate with a paper serviette and glanced furtively around the room. When she was sure no one was looking, she stood up and picked up the plate and fork. But instead of heading for the used crockery table, she sneaked out of the nearest door.

Holly's eyes widened. 'Did you see that?' she hissed. She told Belinda and Tracy what Steffie had just done. Taking food out of the dining-hall was strictly against the rules. 'She must be up to something,' she said. 'Let's go! But don't let her know we're following!'

They scurried towards the door, avoiding a gang of boys from their year and a couple of teachers on dinner duty. Steffie was a good thirty metres ahead and making her way down to D floor, where there was a side exit from the main building.

Tracy, Belinda and Holly hurried on.

'Walk, don't run!' Mrs Bannister, the gym teacher, warned them.

They grimaced and slowed down. Steffie disappeared downstairs, carefully holding the serviette over the dinner plate.

'Where's she going?' Tracy whispered, astonished.

They waited until Mr Simpson had turned a corner towards the staffroom, then broke into a run again. They took the stairs two at a time.

'Which way now?' Belinda asked.

Holly spotted Steffie sneaking through the doors which led out into the covered area where people left their bikes. 'Outside!' she hissed.

They belted through the door, hot on the trail. But Steffie was cautious. She stopped and turned. Holly had to think at lightning speed. 'Jamie!' she yelled, spying her brother out by the bike shed. 'I've got a message for you from Mum!' Belinda and Tracy did their best to fade into the background.

Jamie ambled over, hands in pockets. 'What?' he mumbled.

Steffie, satisfied that no one was following, slipped up the path by the side of the main building.

Holly heaved a sigh of relief. 'Oh, never mind!'

47

she said. And the three of them dashed on. 'I'll explain later!' she called back to her confused brother.

Jamie shrugged and went back to his friends.

They followed Steffie round the side of the school.

'Tracy Foster, just a moment!' a voice called from a ground floor window.

The girls shuddered to another halt.

It was Miss Baron, calling from the music room. 'Can I have a word about changing your violin lesson, please?'

Tracy shrugged and rolled her eyes to the heavens. 'I'll catch up with you later,' she whispered and went off reluctantly to talk to the teacher.

That left Holly and Belinda pretending not to follow Steffie and her lunch. Belinda sighed. 'This is crazy!' she said.

'Yes, but where is she taking it, for goodness sake?' Holly said.

By now Steffie was halfway up the drive and glancing back every few seconds. Holly and Belinda had to dive behind a laurel bush with split-second timing. 'That was close!' Holly said.

'Holly Adams! Belinda Hayes!' Another voice interrupted their chase.

Guiltily, Holly and Belinda stood clear of the bush. It was Miss Earnshaw, wandering down towards them from the main entrance. Holly

clicked her tongue, shrugged and whispered out
of the corner of her mouth, 'That's that, then!' She
glanced up the drive one last time, but Steffie had
already made a clean getaway. Holly waited for
Miss Earnshaw to descend.

'Whatever are you two up to, skulking in the
bushes?' the home economics teacher asked, half
amused, half suspicious.

'Looking for something,' Holly said, squeezing
to the very edge of truth.

'Didn't you hear the bell?' Miss Earnshaw asked.

'No, miss!' they said together.

'What exactly are you looking for? And why do
you keep glancing away like that? What on earth
is wrong with you?'

'Nothing, miss!'

'Well, you'd better get off to registration, then.'
Miss Earnshaw sighed. 'And stop hiding in bushes,
for goodness sake! Girls of your age!' She gave
them one last curious look and sent them back
into school.

Holly and Belinda trailed in. 'I'm fed up with chas-
ing people around school,' Belinda complained.

'Especially when they keep on getting away!'
Holly agreed. Steffie and her lunch would have
to remain a mystery.

That afternoon Mr Lupton sent a message that
Winformation was ready at last. Holly collected a

pile of copies during her break and took them down to Steffie's desk. 'Mr Lupton couldn't find you at the end of lunch-break,' she said pointedly. 'So he had to give the message to me instead.'

Steffie's face didn't even flicker. 'That's fine,' she said. 'I'll send some first years up to collect the rest.' She got busy counting out copies of the magazine. 'Who'd believe that tomorrow is the deadline for the next issue!' She sighed. 'We had to bring it forward this week because of half-term.' She was her normal, brisk self. 'What have you got by way of mystery pages?' she asked Holly.

In her unflagging enthusiasm for the magazine, Holly forgot about the disappearing lunch and dived straight into describing the questionnaire she wanted to do. 'Questions like, "Who is your favourite detective?" and, "Name the best villain in any mystery book you've read."' She paused. 'I'd like to illustrate it with pictures of Sherlock Holmes and Miss Marple and other famous detectives.'

Steffie nodded. 'Good idea. I think these features could work really well if we make them regular.'

Holly soaked up the praise. 'Great!' she exclaimed. 'See you tomorrow!' And she floated out of the library with her pile of magazines, a smile splitting her face almost in two.

Next morning at break, Holly was first to arrive at the *Winformation* desk. She clutched her carefully prepared questionnaire for the mystery pages and looked round for Steffie. She'd managed to persuade both Tracy and Belinda to keep up their help on the school magazine. 'It really will be a way of getting to the bottom of this affair,' she'd promised. 'We have to stick around Steffie as much as possible.'

'Like glue!' Tracy promised.

'Oh boy, more hard work!' Belinda grumbled. 'More typing, more word counting. I don't know if my poor brain can cope!'

But they had both agreed to meet up as before.

'No Steffie?' Tracy asked as she breezed in.

'No, there's no sign of her and it's deadline day for next week's articles.' Holly glanced at the folders and envelopes accumulating on the editor's desk. 'I don't think she's ill, is she?'

'Nope. I saw her during assembly this morning.' Belinda had strolled in, chewing a Mars bar. 'She was definitely here.'

'Then where is she now?' Holly checked that Steffie hadn't collected any of the work on her desk. 'She always turns up here at break, especially on deadline day!'

Tracy made herself comfortable in the editor's chair. 'Maybe she got sick all of a sudden?' she suggested. 'She's sure been acting strange lately!'

Holly nodded and considered the possibility.

'I'll go check the sickroom!' Tracy volunteered. She sprang to her feet.

'And the office. See if she's signed herself out,' Belinda suggested. 'Are you really worried about her?' she asked Holly.

Holly watched absent-mindedly as Tracy took the library steps in a couple of bounds. 'It's pretty well unheard of for Steffie not to be here. And she didn't mention anything unusual yesterday afternoon when I was in here.'

They sat and waited impatiently for Tracy to reappear. She came back, just as another messenger arrived at the *Winformation* desk.

'Mr Greenwood wants to know where Steffie Smith is. She was supposed to turn up ten minutes ago for her French oral test,' the boy said.

Belinda shrugged. 'If we knew where Steffie was, we'd tell you, believe me!'

'Well, she's not sick, and she hasn't signed out!' Tracy announced. It had proved easy to check both the sickroom and the office.

Holly stared at her two friends as the news sank in. 'She was here earlier. She's not sick. She's missed a French test,' she repeated slowly. 'And no one knows where she is?'

Tracy shook her head. 'I asked around. The last anyone saw of her was on her way out of assembly. She never showed up for first lesson.'

Holly stood up. 'Tell Mr Greenwood we don't

know where she is,' she told the boy. He backed out of the room. 'She can't just vanish!' she said, trying to be calm and logical. But memories of Sharon Hall and her flashy silver car and smart driver kept disturbing her efforts. Somehow she felt this was all their fault. 'We should have followed up that Megaware business,' she said to Tracy and Belinda.

'How could we? Steffie said there was nothing wrong!' Belinda reminded her.

'But there is now,' Holly said. 'There's something very wrong!' Her words sank into a tense silence. She strode to the door. 'Hold the fort here for a bit, will you?' she asked. 'Just stall if anyone else wants to know where Steffie is!'

The other two nodded. 'Where are you going?' Tracy asked.

'To use the phone,' she said grimly. 'I'm going to check Steffie's home number.'

The entrance hall was crowded with kids queuing to ring home. Holly looked at the queue in dismay. Then she spotted Mrs Dodson, the librarian. She ran up to her. 'Could I use the library phone, please, Mrs Dodson? It's urgent!'

'It's really for staff use only,' Mrs Dodson said at first. But then she nodded slowly. 'Press 9 before you dial,' she said.

Holly ran back down the corridor, dodging bodies as she went. 'Any news?' Belinda asked.

She and Tracy joined Holly in the tiny library office.

Holly shook her head. 'Hang on.' She checked in the directory for Steffie's number. 'Smith!' she groaned. 'There are hundreds of them!'

Where are you, Steffie? she said to herself. *Why didn't you tell us what was wrong?* Holly was sure this disappearance wasn't to be taken lightly. The more she thought about it, the more certain she was that something sinister and dangerous was happening.

'Wait!' cried Tracy. 'I'll get the number from Mrs Williams in the office! She's a friend of my mom's,' she explained. She ran off, and was back before Holly had got even halfway down the Smith column. She showed Holly Steffie's number scrawled in ink on the palm of her hand.

'Please be in!' Holly whispered as she punched in the numbers. 'Prove me wrong and let it be something normal and simple!' But she was still afraid as she stood waiting. The phone rang on unanswered.

'No good?' Tracy asked.

Holly shook her head. By now her imagination was working overtime. In her mind's eye, she saw Steffie come out of assembly, unconcerned, busily planning her day. She saw her cross the playground to her first lesson. But she never made it. Instead, Holly saw the dark-haired man, the

54

silver car, and Steffie struggling to escape. She imagined Sharon Hall holding the car door open. Steffie was dragged in. Clunk, the door shut! There was Steffie's face behind the smoked glass. And then the car was gone; ghosted away!

She shook her head again, hard this time. She put down the receiver and sighed.

'What now?' Belinda asked.

Holly looked at her watch. Break ended in three minutes. She had to make a quick decision. 'Sign me out at the office,' she told Belinda. 'Say I've gone home with a headache!'

Belinda opened her mouth to protest.

'Hey, that's a bit risky!' Tracy said. She tried to catch hold of Holly's arm.

Holly nodded. 'I know. But it's a risk I'll have to take!' She was already on her way, down the back stairs to D floor. 'I'll borrow Jamie's bike!'

'Where are you going?' Belinda and Tracy broke into a run to keep up.

'Over to Steffie's place. She lives out past the ice rink, doesn't she?' She pulled her brother's bike from its stand. 'Good job he doesn't lock it up!' she said. 'Dad will kill him!'

The others gave her a brief smile. 'Be careful, Holly!' Tracy said. Then she added. 'The address is 32 Dale View, OK? I checked in the file.'

Holly grinned. 'Great, thanks!' She set off up the slope on to the drive. 'I'll be back as soon as I can!'

It would take ten minutes to get to Steffie's house. But what she would find when she got there, she had absolutely no idea!

Steffie's home was a modern house in the new estate set back from the main road out of Willow Dale, just past the ice rink. It was a quiet house in a quiet neighbourhood.

Holly leaned her bike against the low front wall and looked up and down the street. There was no one around. A long-haired, white cat leaped from gatepost to wall, two houses along. She could hear a phone ringing unanswered in the distance.

The garden was like any garden; neat front lawn, roses, a flower border. Holly went up and rang the bell. No answer. She went cautiously down the side of the house to the garage and peered in through a small side window. Greg Smith's extraordinary red car sat gleaming in the very ordinary garage of number 32.

Strange! Holly thought. *I suppose he could have hired a private helicopter and gone off to his Scottish island. But I doubt it!* Her suspicions deepened.

She went round to the back of the house. She cupped both hands around her eyes to cut out the reflection, and put her face against the window. Inside, several newspapers lay scattered on the beige carpet, an empty coffee cup sat on a small table. There was a photograph of Steffie in a silver frame on a bookcase, and a computer on the desk.

'Hey, what are you doing!' a voice cried.

Holly shot backwards and tripped against a tub of geraniums. She looked up over the fence at Steffie's next-door neighbour!

'I said, what are you up to?' the neighbour demanded. She was just tall enough to peer over the fence; a slight old lady with permed hair and a fierce voice.

'I – I'm looking for Steffie Smith!' Holly gasped.

'You look suspicious to me.' The old lady fixed her with a steely glare. 'I think I'd better phone the police!' Her grey head disappeared from view.

'Oh, no, don't do that, please!' Holly dashed across the garden. 'I'm worried about Steffie, that's all. I just came to check if she was here!'

The woman hesitated and turned. 'What are you worried about her for? Isn't she at school?' She eyed Holly's uniform. 'Are you a friend?'

Holly gulped. 'Yes. No, she's not at school!' she said, hardly able to make sense.

The woman approached the fence again. 'That's odd.' She stared at Holly. 'This is a decent neighbourhood. We keep an eye on things for each other!'

'That's good!' Holly gabbled. 'You're sure you didn't see Steffie come back home this morning?'

'No, like I said, this is all very odd. I saw her set

off. Why?' The old lady still looked as though she had police on her mind. 'What's the matter?'

Holly took a deep breath. 'I don't know. But you say there was something odd? Did Steffie do anything unusual? Did she leave at her normal time, for instance?'

The neighbour nodded. 'Normal time, yes.' She thought for a moment. 'Normal route, no.'

Holly grasped the top of the fence. 'Can you tell me what you mean?'

'Well, I was dusting round the front room at about half past eight. That's my first job in the morning. And I happened to look out to see a car I'd never seen before pulling up next door at the Smiths' house!'

'What sort of car, do you remember?'

'Posh, I remember that. A silver thing.'

Holly closed her eyes and tried to keep her head clear. 'Then what?'

'Then a woman got out and tottered up to the front door in those high heels.'

'Did she have red hair?' Holly interrupted.

The woman nodded. 'She rang the bell. Well, I knew Steffie hadn't left for school, so I was surprised when she didn't come to answer the door.'

Holly nodded. 'And then?'

'Well, after a bit the woman went back to the car. She and this chap inside just sat there and waited.'

'For how long?'

'Ages. Maybe they thought Steffie had just popped out on an errand, I don't know. I thought they must have come to give her a lift into school. The woman looked very respectable.'

'She does,' Holly agreed. 'So what did Steffie do?'

'By this time I was feeling a bit awkward peeking out of the window at them, so I came into the kitchen at the back here.'

Holly nodded again.

The woman slowly pieced things together in her memory. 'From the kitchen window I get a good view of the Smiths' garden. And that's what was odd. Steffie was creeping out the back way, through those patio doors. She ran down the length of the lawn; and the silly thing climbed right over that fence there, across the neighbour's garden at the back of us, and out into the next street! I just couldn't understand it!'

'Did the people in the car see her?'

'I don't think so. They were still out front in the car when I took the milk bottles out five minutes later. Then they must have given up and driven off. Next time I looked, they were gone.'

The old lady finished her story and looked curiously at Holly. 'Young Steffie's not gone and played truant, has she?'

'No,' Holly said. 'I'm sure she hasn't.' If only

it were that simple! The neighbour had given her the worst possible news. Sharon Hall had been prowling round here. She'd once been Greg's girlfriend, and she would know where his house was, of course. What's more, Steffie was too scared of her even to answer the door!

Quickly Holly made another decision. She thanked the next-door neighbour and ran for her bike. She pedalled hard down the main road, back into town, hoping she'd be back at school for the last lesson before lunch. And when she got there she was heading straight for the headteacher's office!

5 Motorway mystery

Miss Horswell listened carefully to Holly. She tapped the desk lightly with the end of her pen.

'I've checked everything I can possibly think of!' Holly told her. 'But when I found out from the next-door neighbour that Steffie was too scared even to answer the door to this Sharon Hall woman, I knew things were really serious. So I came to you!' She was still breathless from her bike ride.

'And now Steffie's vanished, you say?' Miss Horswell put her head to one side and studied Holly's face. 'Are you telling me that you think she's been kidnapped?

Holly nodded. She got out of her seat and paced up and down on Miss Horswell's patterned rug. 'Yes! By Sharon Hall and the man in the silver car!' Now that the headteacher had put her own fears into words, Holly felt suddenly cold and shaky.

'Right!' Miss Horswell said briskly. 'The false name of Susan Haigh which she gave to me when we spoke on the phone is especially worrying, if what you say is true. All things considered, I think we'd better get straight on to the police!' She picked up the phone to speak to her secretary.

Holly sat down again. She was sure she was doing the right thing for Steffie, but her legs were trembling anyway. She felt confused.

'Oh, and bring in a cup of tea, please,' Miss Horswell finished. She put down the phone. 'You look as if you need it,' she said.

Holly looked miserably at the headteacher. She felt as if she could confide in Miss Horswell, sitting there in her neat, checked suit, with her grey hair swept tidily back. 'I feel that I should have been able to stop this happening!' she said. 'When I first heard about Steffie's brother and the row over his computer game, and when I saw her acting so strangely, and especially when I suspected Sharon Hall of being up to no good, I should have done something!'

Miss Horswell looked kindly at her. 'You have done something now,' she said. She glanced over Holly's head out of the window.

'Yes, but it's too late. Steffie's already been kidnapped!' Holly said.

'You weren't to know.' Miss Horswell stood up. 'And to be quite frank, Holly, I should have followed up that strange visit to school by Miss Hall myself. I remember I was surprised when she pressed so hard for an appointment, I must say.'

She shook her head. 'Too much to do, I'm afraid.' She looked out of the window again.

Anxious minutes ticked by. At last the head-teacher looked out again and said, 'Here are the police now!' She went out to meet them, leaving Holly alone.

'Tea?' Mrs Williams, the secretary, slipped in and offered Holly the drink. Holly had only taken two sips when the room filled up with Miss Horswell, a grey-haired man in a green zip-up jacket and a uniformed policewoman.

'Holly, this is Detective Sergeant Wilson and Police Constable Jones,' Miss Horswell said quietly. 'I've given them an outline of what's been happening. Now they want to ask you some questions.' She sat at her desk.

Holly smiled faintly at the police officers. She was aware of Miss Horswell willing her to stay calm, and she felt strongly that she mustn't let the headteacher down. She had to do everything she could to help the police find Steffie.

'Now, Holly.' Sergeant Wilson sat down in a seat next to her. He leaned forward to rest his elbows on his knees. 'We need more information. Is there anything at all you can tell us that you haven't thought of so far?'

Holly racked her brains. 'The man driving the car was well-built and well-dressed,' she said. 'I'd say he was in his twenties.'

PC Jones jotted things down as Holly spoke. 'But I didn't get a very good view of him, I'm afraid.'

Sergeant Wilson nodded encouragement. 'That's fine. Just think carefully. Is there anything else?'

In her mind, Holly pictured the car doing its U-turn and speeding off down the hill. 'Yes!' she cried. 'The registration number! It's PC100!'

'Are you sure?' the policeman said quietly.

How could she forget? 'Absolutely!'

Sergeant Wilson nodded at PC Jones. 'Get it checked out, will you?' The woman went quickly out of the room. 'That's great,' he told Holly. 'We'll have it traced in no time!'

Holly sighed. The waves of fear for Steffie's safety were receding. With the police here tracking down Sharon Hall's car, surely the kidnappers couldn't get far!

'Now, was anyone else involved in sighting this car?' Sergeant Wilson proceeded methodically.

'Tracy Foster and Belinda Hayes,' Holly answered promptly.

Miss Horswell stood up. 'I might have guessed!' she said, smiling. 'Do you want me to have them brought along?' she asked the sergeant.

'Yes, please. It's possible they'll remember something else useful, although Holly has already given us a good lead,' he said.

Swiftly, Tracy and Belinda were sent for. They

came into Miss Horswell's room and looked nervously towards Holly. The headteacher introduced them to the sergeant and then sat down patiently at her desk. She smiled encouragingly at all three girls. 'Now, there's no need to worry,' she said. 'It seems Holly was right about Steffie's disappearance being suspicious. The police are following it up now.'

'Are you OK?' Tracy checked quietly with Holly.

Holly nodded. 'Except for being worried stiff about Steffie!' she said. Waiting for news was sometimes worse than having lots to do. So, to keep her fears in check, she took out the Mystery Club's red notebook from her pocket and began to bring it up to date.

'Belinda and Tracy,' Sergeant Wilson began. 'What we want to hear from you is anything at all you can remember about this Miss Hall or Miss Haigh, and the driver of the car. Anything that you think might help!' He sat back and waited, looking quizzically at them.

Tracy began. She described the car they'd seen Sharon Hall getting into. She described the tall, well-dressed figure of the woman herself. Once she was in her stride, she seemed to lose her nervousness and was able to give the sergeant plenty of detail. 'I noticed she moved pretty quickly, and she knew her way about. She had to get down that corridor and out of sight before we made it out of the library. And nothing seemed to bother her. I guess she thinks she could con her way out of anything!' Tracy paused. Her face had come alive and it was difficult for the sergeant to keep up with her description as he jotted down notes.

'Fine!' Sergeant Wilson said appreciatively. He sat there, pen poised. 'I only wish all my own officers were as much on the ball as you three seem to be!' He turned to Belinda. 'Now, there was a driver along with Miss Hall, I hear. What about him?'

Belinda coughed, and shifted awkwardly from foot to foot.

'Go on, Belinda!' Holly whispered. She knew that it might take her longer than Tracy to warm up.

'Well, I'd say he was well-built,' she began. 'He had dark hair.' She stopped to recall the picture of the man as he sped downhill. 'He wasn't scruffy. In fact, he was the opposite,' she said slowly.

'Meaning what?' the sergeant prompted.

'Meaning he was very well-groomed, I suppose. He looked like the men my dad has business meetings with; the most expensive kind of haircut, the best shirts. That kind of thing. Anyway, he certainly didn't look like the ordinary man in the street!'

The sergeant nodded again. 'Thank you, that's very helpful.' He looked up at Miss Horswell. 'You know, these girls are really very observant.' He closed up his notebook and put it back in the top pocket of his jacket. 'Most witnesses get in a muddle about something as simple as the colour of a suspect's hair. First they tell you it's black, then brown, or maybe even blond with an auburn tinge!' He laughed.

The three girls glowed with pleasure.

Miss Horswell looked at her watch. 'How much longer?' she asked Sergeant Wilson.

'Who knows?' He shrugged an apology. 'We'll just have to be patient,' he added.

But half an hour seemed endless as they sat in the teacher's office waiting for news. Bells went for lunch-break, the corridors erupted into noise and bustle, but it all seemed to Holly to happen in a different world.

At last the policewoman returned. They all looked up. Was the waiting over at last?

PC Jones handed a slip of paper to the sergeant. She smiled briefly at Holly.

Sergeant Wilson read the paper and nodded. 'We've traced the car,' he said. 'Motorway police spotted the registration after PC Jones set up the alert. They followed it to a service station. They're holding it until we get there.'

He stood up at once, ready to go. 'How do you feel about a ride with us?' he asked Holly. 'We may need you to identify these people.'

'What about Steffie?' she demanded. 'Is she OK?'

Sergeant Wilson put a steadying hand on her shoulder. 'Hang on. We know there were three people in the car and one of them answers the description Miss Horswell gave us of Steffie. That's all we know. We'll have to wait and see.'

Holly looked at Belinda and Tracy and took in the news slowly. Steffie was there! They'd found her! 'Is it OK if I go?' she asked Miss Horswell.

The headteacher gave her a wry smile. 'Since when did you need my go-ahead on any of your investigations, Holly Adams!'

So Holly found herself in a police car in the early afternoon, riding smoothly towards the motorway, listening to the radio messages being relayed between Sergeant Wilson and the police station. They negotiated city underpasses and sliproads, and finally eased on to the motorway. 'Won't be long now!' PC Jones turned to Holly from the front passenger seat and smiled.

Holly smiled back. It seemed as if things were working out really well after her emergency dash back to school. She pictured meeting a shocked but grateful Steffie at the service station. Sharon Hall and her smooth accomplice would be charged with kidnap and neatly driven off to the nearest station. Then Steffie would be free to tell her everything! Holly felt herself relax as the police car sped towards the service station.

'OK?' Sergeant Wilson asked. He'd signalled to come off the motorway and was driving up the lane leading to a big new motel behind the petrol station. 'They're being held in a private room next to the motel manager's office. Are you all set?' he said to Holly.

She nodded. The car stopped and they all got out. Passers-by gave casually curious glances as Holly and the two police officers walked in through the motel doors.

The manager greeted them and showed them the way, discreet and anxious. 'This way!' he said.

Holly followed down a corridor of ocean-blue carpet.

'In here,' the manager said. Two policemen stood guard outside a closed door. One opened the door into a room with light blue walls and the same dark blue carpet.

The sergeant thanked him and closed the door again firmly. 'Sharon Hall?' he asked in an official, detached voice.

Sharon Hall was sitting cross-legged on one of the soft, blue chairs. She wore a silky, cream blouse. Her hair was twisted back and up on to the top of her head to show gold earrings and matching necklace. She looked cool and poised as usual. 'Yes, I'm Sharon Hall,' she replied.

Holly switched her attention from Sharon to Steffie, who sat across at the far side of the room, nervously twisting a ring on the second finger of her right hand. Steffie refused to meet Holly's gaze. She looked smaller; scared and a bit lost. She kept quiet as the sergeant tried to establish who was who.

'And where's your driver?' Sergeant Wilson asked with a touch of irritation.

'He went to the men's room,' came the calm reply. Sharon Hall studied her fingernails.

Sergeant Wilson looked as if he would go to the two uniformed men outside the door for confirmation, but before he had a chance to act, the driver came back through an inner door behind Sharon Hall. He dried his hands on a paper towel, then pulled the cuffs of his shirt neatly into place. He was of medium height and build, Holly noticed, and, as Belinda had said, very well-groomed. His dark hair was brushed back, he wore a crisp pale blue shirt and dark trousers, immaculately pressed. He looked long and hard at Holly, then introduced himself to Sergeant Wilson.

'I'm Tom Stone,' he said. 'We've been held in this room for more than an hour, and we would like to know what's going on here!'

Holly went and joined Steffie on her side of the room. Tiny alarm bells had begun to ring inside her head. These two certainly weren't acting as though they just been caught kidnapping someone! Still she got no reaction from Steffie.

'We've reason to believe that you and Miss Hall went to the Winifred Bowen-Davies School in Willow Dale earlier today to see Miss Smith,' the sergeant began.

'Sure. Why not?' Tom Stone was insultingly casual. He stood behind Sharon Hall's chair and groomed his hair with his fingertips.

'We also think that you tried and failed to find Miss Smith earlier in the day, before she left home.'

'Right again!' Tom admitted.

'And that once you found Miss Smith at school, you took her from the premises without her consent. In other words, that you abducted the young lady!' Sergeant Wilson concluded.

Sharon Hall gave a sharp dismissive laugh; 'Ha!'

The policeman went on. 'There's plenty of evidence to support the charge. You've been seen snooping round both the house and the school. Miss Smith has been visibly scared by your presence. We understand that she escaped from you early this morning by climbing a fence and running away across a neighbour's garden!' For a moment, Wilson glanced at Holly. She nodded. 'This is a serious charge. Kidnapping!' he challenged.

'Why? Why in the world would we want to kidnap anybody?' Sharon Hall protested, uncrossing her legs and standing up. She was as tall as Sergeant Wilson and met his gaze eye-to-eye.

'That's for you to tell us, or for us to find out,' he said calmly. 'But I must warn you that you needn't say anything without the presence of a solicitor, but that what you do say may be used in evidence—'

'Oh, for goodness sake!' Sharon Hall interrupted. 'If there's a kidnap, there has to be a victim, doesn't there?' She pointed at Steffie. 'Ask her! Go on, ask Steffie!'

Holly, closer to Steffie than anyone else in the room, saw her tremble as her name was mentioned. Steffie's short blonde hair fell forward like a curtain as she bowed her head. She still fiddled with the ring on her finger.

'Go on, Steffie!' Holly breathed. 'You're safe now. You can tell the truth!'

She watched as Steffie bit her bottom lip to stop it trembling. She saw her raise her arm and push back the curtain of fair hair that shaded her face. Her pale blue eyes were wide and staring. Steffie took a deep breath, but no words came out.

PC Jones came over and spoke gently. 'You understand, we want to arrest these two people for kidnapping you? You're not in any danger. Everything's going to be all right!' She reached out and put an arm round Steffie's shoulder.

But Steffie freed herself and sprang to the middle of the room. 'Will people stop going on about me being kidnapped!' she cried. 'I wasn't kidnapped. I chose to go with them!'

She swung round and looked accusingly at Holly. 'It's all your fault!' she shouted. 'Why can't you keep your nose out of things?'

Holly felt the room swim and she clutched the sides of her chair. She couldn't believe what she'd just heard! She felt all the colour drain from her face as she plunged into confusion.

'You see!' Sharon Hall said, calm as ever. 'Who ever heard of a kidnap without a victim!'

'Are you sure?' PC Jones approached Steffie again. 'You're not under any pressure to tell us this, are you?'

Holly saw Steffie flinch and look up at the ceiling. But she denied it. 'No, of course not! Look, I know I shouldn't have left school like that. We're not supposed to. But Sharon offered to take me to a computer show in London. It's the final day. So I just said yes. I didn't know it would cause all this trouble!'

'A computer show?' Sergeant Wilson said slowly.

'At Earls Court.' Sharon Hall picked up her bag and slung it over her shoulder as if everything was clearly sorted out to everyone's satisfaction.

Sergeant Wilson glanced at PC Jones and gave an almost invisible shrug. 'You went of your own free will?' he asked Steffie again.

Steffie nodded.

Holly watched as Sharon Hall went up to the

sergeant. 'You know how young girls are,' she said pleasantly. 'It's a case of an overactive imagination at work here.' She glanced at Holly and put a hand out to shake with Sergeant Wilson to show there were no hard feelings.

'Let's go!' Tom Stone cut in. He stood impatiently by the door.

'I take it you have finished with us?' Sharon Hall said. 'There are no charges?'

Wilson looked at Holly and Steffie one last time. 'No charges,' he confirmed. 'OK everyone, let's shut up shop here and be on our way!'

Tom Stone was gone from the room before the sergeant had finished his sentence. But Sharon Hall paused to give Holly a quick, unmistakable look of triumph. Then she too was gone.

Holly saw Steffie sag and put one hand across her eyes. 'Steffie!' she pleaded. It still wasn't too late! This had all gone horribly wrong; Sharon Hall and Tom Stone had walked free, but they'd left a dozen unanswered questions.

'Leave me alone!' Steffie said, shaking her head. 'I don't even want to talk to you!'

'Now listen,' PC Jones said. 'There's no point you two arguing!' She lowered her voice. 'You'll just have to hope that the sergeant doesn't think you've been wasting police time!' she told Holly.

Sergeant Wilson had checked off a few details

with the two men at the door, but now he came back in, his face stern.

Holly felt dreadful; about a centimetre tall and ready to dissolve into tears. But she held her head up.

Wilson sniffed and looked from Holly to Steffie and back again. 'Playing truant is one thing,' he told Steffie. 'It's not a criminal offence. But deliberately misinforming the police is!' He stared Holly in the face. 'In any case, I don't want to have this sort of thing happening again. Understand?'

Holly nodded. She saw PC Jones give her a little wink from behind Sergeant Wilson's back, but her kindness only made it all feel worse somehow. Holly looked down miserably at her feet.

'You'd better hop in the car and we'll drive you back to school,' he grumbled. He looked at his watch. 'Come on, look sharp!'

The police car arrived back at school just as the final bell of the day rang. Kids poured out of doors into the playground, up the drive, across the playing-fields. A few of them gathered around the car as Steffie and Holly stepped out.

'Holly!' Tracy pushed through the crowd to the front. 'Are you OK? What happened?'

Holly tried to smile and nod. She could see Belinda pushing from the back to reach her. The noise and chaos almost got the better of her, until teachers came and cleared everyone off.

Then PC Jones ushered her and Steffie into Miss Horswell's room and Holly had no time to explain to her friends. The headteacher looked serious. She listened to the policewoman in silence.

'That's about it, I'm afraid.' PC Jones finished her account. 'They're lucky that the sergeant realises that Holly's motives weren't malicious. But he wants the girls to understand that they mustn't do anything like this again.'

'Oh dear!' Miss Horswell sighed. 'I'm afraid I may be as much to blame here as anyone. Still, I do agree; it mustn't happen again!' She went and showed the policewoman out. 'As for you girls,' she said when she came back, 'I'll need time to work out what action I should take.' She seemed sad and disappointed.

Holly felt her heart sink to its lowest point ever. She was too upset even to speak.

'So, I won't do anything hasty.' Miss Horswell arranged papers on her desk and settled her glasses on her nose. She looked up. 'Let's leave it until first thing in the morning, shall we?' And she dismissed them with a brief nod.

Out in the corridor, Belinda and Tracy pounced.

'What happened? We want to know every single detail!' Tracy exclaimed. 'Are you OK, Steffie? Hey, what's wrong?'

To Holly's amazement, Steffie's face was streaming with tears. 'Oh God!' she sobbed. She broke free of

Belinda as she tried to comfort her. She ran through the main doors and blindly up the drive.

'What's going on?' Belinda said. 'It's something terrible, isn't it?'

Holly nodded. 'Really terrible. I don't know what it is, but it must be pretty awful.' She gazed up the drive. The beech trees rippled in the quiet breeze. A squirrel scrambled down one trunk and over the smooth lawn. But the drive was deserted. Holly stood there. She felt empty and let down and betrayed!

6 Steffie says sorry

'Holly, you've remembered our arrangements for this evening, haven't you?' Mrs Adams asked next morning at breakfast. 'I'm leaving you our hotel phone number in case you have a crisis, and Mrs Walker from next door will be home the whole time.' She smiled at her daughter.

Holly stared at her orange juice. The feeling of gloom still hovered over her from the day before. 'Mmm,' she mumbled.

'Since it's half-term, we've made plans for Jamie to stay with a friend. You're sure the three of you will be OK here while we're away?' her mother checked. She had on her smartest business suit, ready to leave for her job as manager of one of Willow Dale's banks. 'Are you all right?' she asked. 'You'll be late if you don't get a move on, you know!' She took the car keys from their hook.

'What? Oh yes, I'm fine.' Holly didn't want to bother her mother or father with the Steffie Smith problem and her troubles at school. She didn't want to spoil their wedding anniversary and their short trip away. She made an effort, smiled and gulped down her orange juice. 'Don't worry; everything will be fine here!' She gave her mother a peck on the cheek. 'Have a great time!' she said.

She told her father the same thing when she called in at his workshop across the yard from the house. She was in a hurry, on her way to school. He was busy finishing a commission for an exclusive furniture store in London, a nest of hand-carved and polished tables. 'Enjoy yourselves tonight, Dad!' she said.

'We will.' He looked up from his work. 'And you,' he smiled.

'I will!' Holly set off. If only he knew the trouble she was in! And maybe he would; if Miss Horswell decided to inform her parents about it! She went to school full of worries, knowing that her interview with the headteacher was to happen before school began. She wouldn't even be able to meet up with Tracy and Belinda. No moral support; nothing!

'Now, Holly!' Miss Horswell began, deadly quiet and controlled.

Holly stood in her office before morning registration, dreading the worst.

'I've already spoken to Steffie about yesterday afternoon's little misunderstanding. I've told her that whilst I don't consider a detention suitable punishment for a sixth former, I'm still extremely disappointed in the way that she chose to skip lessons without permission yesterday.' She paused, giving Holly the full force of her gaze.

Holly tried to swallow the lump in her throat. Perhaps she was in trouble deeper than she'd ever been before. She felt her palms go hot and sticky, her throat go dry. It was like waiting for a judge to pass sentence.

'And as for you,' Miss Horswell began. But her voice had softened and she looked more like her normal, kindly self. 'Well, Holly, I really don't know what to say to you!' She paused again. 'How can I put it? I wonder if the time has come for you to carefully reconsider your fascination with mysteries!'

Holly nodded, feeling the colour flood to her cheeks at Miss Horswell's attempt to be tactful.

The headteacher sighed. 'In a way I wish there were more people like you in the world. Wanting to help others is a desirable thing. But . . .' She smiled. 'I feel I must give you a word of advice. Avoid the temptation to see a mystery around every corner! Especially when people might prefer you to mind your own business!'

Holly nodded again, but she felt a terrible urge to stand up for herself. There *was* a mystery about Steffie's disappearance, even if no one else saw it! She just had to recall Steffie's face as she told the police that Sharon Hall hadn't kidnapped her. There had been terror in her eyes!

But Holly knew now was not the time to discuss it. She simply nodded her head. 'I'm sorry,' she said.

Miss Horswell nodded. 'Good. Now, Holly, I'm sure that everything you did yesterday was done from the very best of motives. And you know that I question my own judgement over the matter too.' She placed the palms of her hands together and continued to talk quietly and sensibly. 'I also recognise that you're a girl who's done a lot for Winifred Bowen-Davies since you came to us.' She paused again. 'And I realise that you must have passed a horrible evening yesterday?'

Holly nodded.

'So in the end I think we have to say that this must be the end of the business. No more fuss!' Miss Horswell stood up briskly to bring the interview to an end. 'Let's just get on with our work and forget it ever happened, shall we?'

She smiled brightly as she showed Holly to the door.

Holly backed out of the room feeling a strange mixture of relief and shame. But Tracy and Belinda were right there when she needed them. They met her in the Head's corridor.

'Still in one piece?' Belinda asked.

'Was Steffie in there with you?' Tracy wanted

to know. 'What did she have to say about all this?'

Holly explained as they walked along to registration, and by the time they arrived she felt more like her usual self. 'Let's meet up at the *Winformation* desk at break,' she said. 'There's loads of catching up to do after yesterday's mess!'

'You mean you're not going to drop it?' Tracy asked.

Holly felt them both staring at her, eager for a reply. Miss Horswell's kindly advice was fresh in her mind. 'We'll have to be careful not to get the school caught up in this again,' she said. 'Officially, at least. But as for dropping it; no, I most certainly am not!'

But still, Holly wasn't looking forward to facing up to Steffie again. When she found her at break, busy at her desk, Holly did her best to act normally. 'Hi,' she said, going over to the computer keyboard. 'Are these the pieces that need typing in?' She intended to stick to her promise to help with this week's rushed edition of *Winformation*.

Steffie's face looked paler than usual against her blonde hair, and she looked as if she hadn't had much sleep. But she was calm, concentrating on the work in hand. 'Hi. Yes, there's that article on the school trip to Paris. Could you do that first, please.'

Holly glanced at it, ready to begin. But Steffie

came across to her. She cleared her throat, but still her voice came out muffled. 'I have to tell you something,' she said.

Holly looked up. Her nerves tingled. What was coming next?

'I want to say I'm sorry.' Steffie mumbled. 'What I did to you yesterday wasn't fair, I realise that. I really am sorry.'

Holly took a deep breath. 'That's OK,' she said carefully. 'But I wish you would tell me what was really going on!'

Steffie stepped back. 'I can't do that.'

'Why not?'

'Just because!' Steffie insisted. 'I needed to tell you I was sorry. And thank you for trying to help. But I can't say any more, OK?'

Holly nodded. She would have to be satisfied with that. And Steffie's apology did mean a lot to her. She smiled.

But it had set her thinking again. By the time Belinda and Tracy joined them to see what extra help they could offer, Steffie had slipped off to see Mr Lupton and Holly's brain was working overtime.

'Is everything OK?' Belinda asked. She glanced round the desktop. 'Don't tell me, Super Steffie has got everything totally under control again. The panic's over and you don't need us any more!' She made as if to slide out into the corridor.

'Not so fast!' Tracy protested. She picked up a handful of notices about forthcoming car boot sales, parents' evenings and lost property. She sifted through them. 'Here's a whole heap of stuff for you to sort out!' She thrust the papers into Belinda's hands.

'Why me?' Belinda moaned. But she sat down to help.

'Any more information for our little red book?' Tracy went on. 'Regarding Steffie and the kidnap-that-never-was, I mean.'

Holly looked up. 'She did say sorry.'

'Who, Steffie?'

'Yes. That must be a first. I suppose it's worth writing that down!' Holly smiled, but she wasn't really in the mood for jokes.

Belinda took it up. 'If she apologised, isn't that the same as admitting you were right yesterday, Holly?' She'd turned from her task and bit her lip thoughtfully.

'Right about Sharon Hall and that man,' Tracy agreed. 'So what do we do now?'

Holly shook her head. 'For some reason, Steffie is still denying it all.'

Tracy tapped her pencil against the desk. 'Let's think. Let's see if we can get ahead in this little game they're playing!'

'Difficult,' Holly pointed out.

'And not so little,' Belinda reminded them.

'SPACE WALK and MOON MAZE are worth millions, remember!'

'How could we forget?' Tracy went over and perched by Holly. 'What do you think?' she asked.

Holly looked up. 'Like I say, it's hard to make a plan until we get to the bottom of Steffie's strange behaviour. That's what we have to do.' She sighed and looked at her two friends in turn. 'Tell me something. Miss Horswell accused me of having a fascination with mysteries. Do you think she's right?'

Tracy and Belinda laughed out loud.

'Yes, thank heavens!' Belinda said.

'And it's contagious, like measles. Now we all have it!' Tracy agreed.

'Good!' Holly grinned. 'Tell me, doctor, is there any cure?'

Tracy bent forward, elbows on the desk. 'I'm afraid not, Miss Adams. What you have is a bad case of Mystery Clubitis!'

'Oh no!' Holly fell back in her chair.

'Listen you two, are there two "m"s in "accommodation"?' Belinda asked. She'd gone back to proofreading an article. 'Or one "m" and two "c"s? Or one "m" and one "c"?'

'Two of everything,' Holly said absent-mindedly. In her head she was already sifting through the clues to Steffie's mystery once again.

Then the bell went and work had to stop. Lessons

always called them away from the really important things in life!

It was during music class that the stroke of luck Holly needed happened, though it didn't feel like it at the time.

'I need three girls and three boys to help move equipment into the fifth form centre for tonight's Year 9 concert!' Miss Baron announced. She looked round the room. 'Luther, Mark, Kurt; will you help, please? And Tracy, Belinda and Holly; you three!'

They all stood up and made their way downstairs to the centre, where they began to move lights and speakers into position, ready for the evening's performance.

Tracy enjoyed working alongside Kurt Welford. He was fun when they went out together, and he made a good atmosphere whenever there was a job to do; easy-going and sensible. He knew how the lights worked and set about getting the right lamps for each bracket. 'This red one goes here,' he said from the top of a ladder. He fixed it tightly in place. 'Hey, has anyone got a spare blue filter for this one?'

'Here.' Tracy climbed halfway up the ladder with the blue plastic disk. 'Are you working the lighting-board for them tonight?' she asked.

Kurt nodded. 'Miss Baron roped me in as usual.'

Tracy grinned. 'Bad luck. How does this light fit on to this stand?' she asked.

Belinda showed her how it worked. 'This goes on here like this!' she demonstrated, as if to a three year old. 'There, now you try!'

They worked seriously for a few more minutes before it was necessary for Holly to go to the store by the bike shed to fetch more stands. She went off alone.

Just as she emerged from the dark store, she stopped short. Steffie Smith was crossing the yard, using the same route as before out of school.

Something told Holly to stay hidden. This time Steffie wasn't just going to vanish into thin air. There were no teachers around to intercept them, and Holly was determined to find out where she was so keen to sneak off to!

She must have caught her off guard, for Steffie ran quickly up the slope, scarcely glancing to left or right.

What's she doing, slipping off in the middle of a lesson? Holly thought. She caught sight of Belinda and Tracy coming out to the store. She beckoned them quietly and quickly and pointed to Steffie's disappearing figure. 'Ready? Let's follow her!' she said.

They all breathed deeply and ran up the hill, keeping close in to the trees. They followed, but they were ready to dodge sideways to hide. No

87

need; for once Steffie got clear of the school, she headed as fast as she could for the gate without once looking back. Holly and the others easily kept her in sight.

But instead of going straight ahead through the exit and out on to the street with its huge, ivy-covered hotel and grand Victorian houses, Steffie suddenly veered to her left and sneaked down a half-hidden alleyway.

'Why's she going down there?' Tracy said. 'It's the old caretaker's place. No one goes down there!' In fact, it was strictly out of bounds, and almost hidden behind a high privet hedge.

'Come on!' Holly said. She sprinted freely the last twenty metres.

They arrived just in time to hear the gentle click of the door latch at the end of the overgrown path.

'Duck!' Belinda squealed suddenly and without warning.

'Why?' Tracy did as she was told, but she'd ended up with a mouthful of privet leaves. The uncut hedge had provided emergency cover.

Holly peered through the bush and saw the reason for Belinda's panic. A car was cruising slowly past the main gates and two people looked out, scanning the front of the school. 'Sharon Hall!' Holly gasped. 'Surely they're not about to risk setting foot in the place again!' She thought it through. 'Not that I'd put anything past them.'

She felt exasperated by being caught off guard once again.

'I saw them coming down the hill,' Belinda explained. 'Sorry, Tracy!'

'They certainly don't give up, do they?' Tracy said.

'Well, neither do we,' Holly muttered. She knew they were on the very edge of an important discovery. All they had to do was open the boarded-up door of the old caretaker's house, and all would be revealed!

They waited a safe time to let the silver car drive clear of the school, then they crept down the path. It was strewn with dandelions, and nettles grew alongside the step, but Holly pressed on. She pushed the door. It refused to open. 'It's locked from the inside!' she whispered.

Together they crawled quietly to the right, along the front of the house to the nearest window. That was locked too. Holly frowned, then beckoned them on down the side of the house and round the back. Here they found another door. Holly's hopes rose as she crawled forward to try the handle.

But this door held fast too. The girls squatted and considered what to do next. 'I suppose whoever's in there wouldn't be stupid enough to leave the doors and windows unlocked,' Tracy admitted.

'Let's go back round the front!' Holly suggested. They crept on.

'Ah!' Belinda said with a yelp. They'd almost reached the front door by crawling through an overgrown bed of roses and weeds. 'It's the pollen! I'm going to sneeze! Aah!'

At that moment the door opened and Steffie stepped out. Holly seized the chance. Startled by Belinda's sneeze, Steffie stood stock still in the doorway. Holly, with Tracy and Belinda close behind, leaped forward and shoulder-charged up the step.

It was over in a couple of seconds. They bundled Steffie back inside the dark hallway. She sat down hard on the bare boards. Holly stumbled and fell. Too late to stop themselves, Belinda and Tracy landed with a crash on top!

'Oh no!' Steffie groaned. 'Shut the door! Shut it quick!'

Tracy scrambled free to shut it.

Holly and Belinda helped to pick Steffie off the floor. They'd fallen against a stack of half-used paint tins. An old ladder lay lengthways down the hall. As her eyes gradually got used to the dark, Holly made out that the house was used as some sort of storeroom. 'OK?' she asked Steffie. She almost apologised for knocking her over, until she remembered why! 'OK!' she said again. But this time it was a demand for an explanation.

Steffie brushed herself down. 'Oh, all right!' She looked wildly down the corridor and sighed. 'Come in here!' And she led them into a lighter room stacked with broken school chairs and tables.

Holly faced her across the empty space in the middle. She felt tough and unforgiving; Steffie had told them lots of lies and she wasn't going to get away with it again! 'Start talking! Start with yesterday!' she said. 'Sharon Hall did kidnap you, didn't she?'

Steffie sighed again and nodded. 'Yes, all right then, she did! And that awful Tom Stone. If you must know, they did! They were using me to get at Greg. We set off for London, but not to go to a computer show. They were going to keep me hidden there! Until you interrupted their plans!' Her voice rose. 'I said I was sorry, didn't I?'

'That's not enough!' Tracy cut in on Holly's behalf. 'I'd keep talking if I were you!'

Holly walked up to Steffie. She saw that her big, blue eyes were screwed up with fear again, and she could soon fly off into another temper. But this time Holly wouldn't be put off. 'So if they had kidnapped you, why on earth did you tell the police that they hadn't?' she demanded. She stood firm, hands on hips.

'Because!' Steffie wailed. She darted desperate glances around the room.

'Because of me,' a calm voice said from the doorway.

Holly spun round. A tall fair figure stood there in crumpled shirt and trousers. His face was unshaven and he didn't match his glamorous newspaper photograph. But it was Greg Smith!

7   *A piece of blue plastic*

'We'd better all sit down,' Greg Smith suggested. He chose some usable chairs from the stack of broken furniture and offered the first one to his sister. 'You OK?' he asked.

Steffie nodded. 'Sorry!' she said faintly, indicating Holly and the others.

'It's not your fault.' Greg sat down on the last chair. 'No one saw you come down the alleyway, did they?' he asked Holly.

Holly shook her head. 'Sharon Hall is still prowling around though!'

Greg frowned. 'Will I ever get rid of that woman?' he said with surprising force. He leaned forward to pat Steffie's hand. 'It's OK, I won't do anything stupid,' he promised.

It took Holly a while to take in this new picture of things. Here was Steffie's brother, holed up right under their noses in this neglected old building, surrounded by paint and dust. He hadn't fled to some secret island hideaway after all! And Steffie had been lying every step of the way; not just about her kidnap, but about Greg, his business affairs, everything! Holly cleared her throat and tried to concentrate. 'Is this where you've been hiding since you "resigned" from Starware?' she asked.

Greg grinned sheepishly. 'You've got the advantage over me,' he said. 'You seem to know who I am all right, but I don't believe we've ever had the pleasure!' His light brown eyes twinkled as he held out a hand to Holly.

She swallowed hard. 'I'm Holly Adams,' she said.

Belinda wiped the dust from her palm and went forward to shake hands too. 'Belinda Hayes,' she muttered.

Then Tracy sprang forward. 'Hi. I'm Tracy Foster!' She smiled brightly at Greg.

'It's OK, they're friends of mine,' Steffie mumbled ungraciously. 'Holly helps me on the school magazine. But I never expected them to follow me here!' She glared at Holly.

Greg shrugged. 'It's not your fault; don't worry.' Then he turned back to Holly. 'So you didn't believe I'd dropped out?' he asked. 'Well, you were right, of course. And Steffie's been a hero, trying to keep everyone off my back. Even when it meant she was in danger herself!' He looked at his sister and shrugged. 'It's OK, there's no point covering up from these three any more!' he said.

Holly turned to Steffie. 'And it's for some reason

connected with Greg that you couldn't tell the police that Sharon Hall had kidnapped you?' she said, slowly working things out.

Steffie sighed. 'Yes. It was terrible. They grabbed me when I was on my way round the back of the sports hall after assembly yesterday. There was no one else around. That horrible Stone man crept up and put a hand over my mouth. I kicked as hard as I could, but he just dragged me across to the carpark at the bottom entrance and he slung me into the back seat of their car. He kept my head down so no one could see me, and Sharon Hall drove off. I was helpless!'

Holly nodded. 'It sounds as if they'd been planning it for days. But why?'

Steffie looked again at Greg.

'Go ahead, tell them the whole thing. Maybe then we'll get some fresh ideas on what to do next.' He leaned back against the wall. 'I'm tired of thinking!' he said.

Steffie continued, her voice growing stronger and clearer. 'It's not me they wanted, of course. It's Greg! You know they work for Megaware International? Sharon's the one who tried to steal MOON MAZE from the back of Greg's car!'

'Hey, wait a minute!' Tracy broke in and turned to Holly and Belinda. 'Am I hearing this right? Sharon Hall is a kidnapper *and* a thief?'

'*And* an ex-girlfriend?' Holly looked curiously at

Greg, waiting for an explanation.

He nodded. 'The more fool me, you could say. That's right. About three months ago I actually went out with that woman.' He laughed. 'I made the mistake of thinking she really felt something for me!'

Steffie went up to him. 'Never mind. I knew she was trouble, though. She was just too . . . well, too good to be true. And she was always saying how clever you were with SPACE WALK, how you were an absolute genius. It was obvious she wanted something!'

'Not to me.' Greg blushed. 'OK, I was well and truly taken in. I fell for it. I thought we had a lot in common; I knew she worked for Megaware, in the same type of work as me.'

Belinda nodded. 'I can understand that. I bet she was pretty convincing. Why think there was anything wrong?'

'Sure. I was flattered as well. Megaware's been a big name in the computer world, even if they're going through a bad patch right now. When Sharon told me that SPACE WALK was better than anything they'd ever done, I believed her.' He glanced sheepishly at Steffie. 'So I showed her my ideas for a new game that would be even better and bigger than SPACE WALK.'

Steffie crossed her arms. 'Hadn't you ever heard of industrial spies?' she said.

'So now Sharon Hall's a spy, too?' Tracy gasped.

Greg shifted forward from his resting place against the wall, and began to pace about the room, head down, hands in pockets. 'I suppose that's what you'd call her, yes. I remember I was uneasy telling Sharon too much about MOON MAZE, but she really pushed me for information. I was still developing it. I'm still putting the finishing touches to it now, as a matter of fact. Writing the master programme is a complicated business!' He left them and went out of the room for a few moments. When he came back, he was carrying an expensive looking portable computer. He tapped it gently. 'This is where I keep my newest little baby, see!'

'And you say Sharon showed even more interest in this game than in SPACE WALK?' Holly asked.

'Well, she would, wouldn't she?' Steffie put in. 'It was brand new and no one else had seen it.'

Greg shrugged. 'Anyway, finally I cottoned on to the fact that something wasn't right. Sure, she liked the candle-lit dinners and drives in the country. But she was always just a bit too interested in work. She even asked me for a copy of MOON MAZE in its development stage. When I said no, she sulked. That wasn't very pretty, let me tell you. Then I caught her snooping in my office in town, one day when I was late back from a meeting.'

'And even if you didn't listen to me, you finally

had to take notice of Nick,' Steffie reminded him.

He nodded. 'Yes. Nick Powell's my publicity manager. He thought I should cool it with Sharon. He said she could be bad news for Starware.' Greg paused and sighed. 'In the end, I decided to test her out, to set a kind of trap. We were sitting in my car and my PC was on the back seat. I asked her to keep an eye on it while I went to buy a newspaper. "There are millions of pounds worth of programming on that computer, so guard it with your life!" I said. I tried to make it sound like a joke.'

Holly felt sorry for him as he recalled how Sharon had let him down. 'Did she steal it?' she asked. 'Did she steal the half-finished version of MOON MAZE?'

'Let's say she borrowed it. She took the disk from the computer while I went to the shop. It wasn't the genuine master disk, of course.'

'But it did prove she was a spy.' Holly admired the trick.

Greg nodded. 'Like I say, she "borrowed" it for an hour, copied it for Megaware and slipped it back into my PC. But I checked and I knew she'd taken it, even though she denied it.' He took a deep breath. 'I'd like to have been there and seen their faces when they realised I'd substituted a fake.'

'Served them right!' Steffie said. 'Then on top of that, Greg dumped Sharon.'

'"Dumped" is putting it a bit strongly,' he objected. 'I thought I was quite nice about it, considering.'

Holly looked round at Tracy and Belinda. All this was slotting into place. 'I see,' she said slowly. 'Sharon Hall has quite a few reasons to be mad at you!'

'Yes. She hated being "dumped" as Steffie calls it. She nearly went mad, kept calling me at the office and shouting down the phone. Getting rid of her proved more difficult than you'd ever believe,' he said.

'But at least you still had MOON MAZE,' Tracy pointed out. 'And you'd spotted her little game. You won in the end!'

'But the game isn't over yet. I'm winning, for the moment at least,' he corrected her. Greg pressed the eject button on the computer. And, like a magician showing an audience his true hand, he pulled out a small, flat, square blue disk. 'A little more time and this baby will be ready!' he said. 'One or two more days and it will be off my hands. *Finito!*'

'I see!' Tracy said. She went and sat cross-legged on a broken desk and made herself comfortable there. 'So that's the real disk, is it? But why would they want to steal MOON MAZE in the first place? Can't they just buy a copy in any shop?'

'Ah, but this isn't just any old copy!' Greg

explained. 'This is the only disk that contains all my programming and all the work I put into writing and developing the game. If they get hold of this, they can put it on their computers and see exactly how it's written. Then they can copy straight from it.'

Holly nodded slowly. 'With that master disk they can copy as many as they like and sell the game themselves!'

Belinda took off her glasses to peer closely at the ordinary looking piece of blue plastic in Greg's hand. 'You're telling us that this is worth a lot of money?' she breathed.

Greg laughed. 'Yes. Not very pretty to look at, is it?'

'Not exactly the crown jewels,' she admitted. She put her glasses back on and shrugged at Holly.

'Right!' Greg looked round the room to let these ideas sink in. 'It's up-to-date stuff, this. Often the police can't get to grips with it. You just have to understand that it would take Megaware years to develop their own game to rival MOON MAZE! And they don't have years. They're really struggling to keep up with new companies like us. Stealing the disk would be a terrific short cut!'

'So, it's not just a little plastic disk that they tried to get hold of,' Belinda repeated. 'It's stealing an *idea*! And the idea's worth thousands of pounds!'

'Millions!' Steffie reminded them. 'MOON MAZE is going to be the game *everyone* wants!'

Greg blushed and put the disk safely back in his pocket.

Tracy almost bounced off the desk in her excitement. 'So, go on, what exactly happened after you dumped Sharon? And what about the police? What did they do? And how come the newspapers got it wrong about you deciding to drop out?'

'Hey!' Greg laughed and held up his hands in surrender. 'Slow down!'

Holly joined Tracy to perch on the desk. 'You can't blame us for being curious,' she said. There were a dozen loose ends to tie up.

'OK, what happened after you tricked Sharon and dumped her?' Tracy asked again. She tried to stay calm.

Greg took a deep breath. 'After she'd finished yelling at me down the phone, she sent in Tom Stone!'

Holly heard Steffie's sharp, worried intake of breath.

'It only took them twenty-four hours,' Steffie said. 'And it was really scary stuff. They were determined to have the real thing, so they made death threats, everything! All personally delivered by Mr Stone. No phone messages, no letters, or anything that could be used as proof!'

'No, that's not their style,' Greg agreed. 'They're

101

ruthless through and through, these big international companies. The more money they make the greedier they get. I realised that when Stone lay in wait in the carpark in town and shadowed me home late one night. He even tried to drive me off the road.'

The girls looked carefully at one another. Holly realised with a shock just how big and dangerous this crime was. She felt the little hairs at the nape of her neck begin to prickle and she turned to Belinda.

'OK,' Belinda said in her considered way. 'They made all these threats. Now for my question. What about the police? What did they do?'

'They did what they could,' Greg told her. They investigated the theft of the so-called master disk, but of course Sharon had already returned it by then. They brought out the fingerprint man, took down details from me, went off and checked her story when I told them she was the thief.' He paused and a little muscle twitched in his jaw. Holly could see the tension he was living under.

'And?' Belinda said. 'Then what?'

'She gave them an alibi,' Greg said flatly.

'Who from?'

'Tom Stone.'

The three girls gasped in annoyance. Belinda shook her head. 'But he's her accomplice! And you mean to say they believed him?'

102

'What else could they do? There was no hard evidence.' Greg passed one hand wearily across his forehead. 'They left the file open, pending further investigations. But without proof we were sunk.'

'Right,' said Holly in the depressed silence that followed. 'My turn! Like Tracy said, how come the newspapers got it all wrong?'

'Ah!' Steffie stepped in. She was something like her old, brisk self. 'That's my fault, I'm afraid!' She half smiled at them.

Holly laughed. 'You don't look sorry!'

Steffie grinned back. 'Well, no actually! When we got to the point that Greg was well and truly in danger and the police couldn't help, I knew we had to dream up something good!'

'A good smoke-screen,' Greg explained. 'I agreed with Steffie that maybe we could create some confusion to throw Sharon and Stone off my track.'

'Why, what were they doing by this time?' Tracy asked.

Belinda was floating behind them, pacing the room, thinking.

The worried, drawn look returned to Greg's face. His voice dropped. 'One night I came out of the gym face-to-face with Tom Stone down a nasty dark alleyway. He said if I didn't hand over the master disk by lunch-time next day, I was dead meat!' He smiled grimly. 'Let's just say I believed him!'

Steffie broke the silence as Greg paused, deep in

his own thoughts. 'He was able to stall for a bit. He told Stone the disk was no good to Megaware until it was finished. He needed a few more days. And that's when I came up with my idea. I said if Greg wasn't willing to give up the whole thing, we needed to do something drastic. Greg wasn't too sure at first.'

'Is that what you were arguing about the other day in town?' Belinda asked. 'Just before the newspapers broke the story about you resigning?'

Greg and Steffie both blushed. 'Not a very private place, eh?' Greg admitted. 'We were both under a lot of pressure. I said I couldn't just back down and let Megaware get away with it. It wasn't the money; it was the principle! They wanted to steal my property and they were threatening my life! Only a coward would back off from that!'

'So I said he should at least hide the disk and lie low himself,' Steffie went on. 'Vanish somehow, so they would lose track of him. I thought of that false story for the papers!' she said proudly. 'Make Sharon and Tom Stone believe that they really had scared Greg off to some place hundreds of kilometres away, just to confuse them.'

'But in fact I'd lie low in Willow Dale itself, working like crazy to finish the disk and hand it over to Nick.'

Holly understood. 'So you did agree with Steffie? Trying to confuse Sharon was a good thing?'

'It was the best we could do,' he explained. 'And they were still putting on the pressure.'

'So why not really put some distance between yourself and Stone? Why not go off to Scotland, for instance?'

'Too risky,' Steffie explained. 'Stone and Hall were keeping watch practically twenty-four hours a day. They'd have spotted him and followed him, wherever he went!'

'All I wanted to do was finish MOON MAZE, and keep an eye on Steffie here if I could. Of course, Sharon's devious mind realised the newspapers might have got it wrong. No doubt Megaware put out feelers to find my so-called-out-of-the-way hiding-place, but Sharon must have thought her best bet was to stay put and keep up the pressure on Steffie. That's when she started cruising round the school, poking her nose in.'

'Which was the worst thing possible!' Steffie explained. 'Because this was the very place we'd chosen for Greg to hide; somewhere that no one would think of or be able to find! I met him and slipped him in here half an hour after that row you saw in town.' She shook her head. 'It went smoothly, but it turned out that it was the only thing that did. Sharon was impossible to shake off. And now look!' She spread her hands in despair.

'It's been awful for you these last few days, I

know.' Greg came up to Steffie and put an arm around her.

The girls waited while Greg and Steffie got control of themselves. Holly saw how much they meant to each other. 'Steffie did a fantastic job of keeping your secret!' she told Greg. 'It was really hard for us to find out what she was up to!'

'Too much even for the famous Mystery Club!' Steffie teased.

Holly looked at Tracy and Belinda. 'I wouldn't say that,' she argued. 'Not quite!'

'We're here aren't we?' Belinda pointed out. 'But why choose here to hide? This is a grotty old place!' She glanced at the pile of broken chairs and the boarded up window.

'Did *we* think of it?' Tracy said quietly. She prowled about, concentrating, trying to work out what to do next.

Belinda laughed. 'OK, I get the point! I suppose it's a great hiding-place!' she admitted. 'If only Sharon hadn't been so sharp about your every move.'

Holly was also thinking her way from one idea to the next. 'Yes, but I think we need another plan now,' she said. 'The police seem to have been tied in knots by Sharon's false alibis, so it really is up to us if we want to keep Greg and his disk out of their greedy hands!' She turned back to face Greg. 'Look, before we decide what to do next, I just want to clear up one more thing!'

Greg raised his hands. 'Shoot!' he joked.

'Don't!' Steffie shuddered. 'Not even in fun.'

Greg lowered his hands. 'OK, sorry. What is it?'

'It's a question for Steffie, really,' Holly said. 'When Sharon Hall and Tom Stone kidnapped you, what did they say?'

'To stop me from telling the truth, you mean?' Steffie paused. 'It's hard to remember the order things happened in, I was so scared. Well, first they told me they'd sent a ransom demand to Nick at Starware's office. No, not for money. No, the demand said that if he didn't contact Greg to hand over the master disk they'd kill me!' She lowered her head and found it hard to carry on. 'I didn't know whether to believe them. There we were speeding down the motorway towards London in the fast lane, with Sharon Hall driving. She has a flat near Earls Court. Stone was telling me he wouldn't hesitate to kill me if necessary!' She started to tremble again at the memory. 'It was a nightmare!'

'Then what?' Holly asked gently.

'Then a police car came past, flashing its blue light. They pulled us on to the hard shoulder. I wanted to cry with relief. I thought I was safe!'

'It's OK,' Greg comforted her. 'Take your time!'

She nodded and began again. 'But just before the policeman came over to speak to us and ask us to follow him to the motel at the services, Sharon turned round to me. She said, "If you say one word here, you're dead!" Then she turned round to wind down the window and speak to the policeman. Stone was still in the back with me,' Steffie whispered. 'He said to me, "The story is that you agreed to come with us, OK?" And I said yes! They were going to kill me!' she cried.

'Steffie, I'm so sorry!' Greg said. He looked at Holly. 'Maybe I *should* give it all up and hand over the master disk.' He sighed. 'I can't have my kid sister going through any more of this for me, can I?'

But Steffie jumped in before Holly could answer. 'No, not now!' she cried. 'Not after we've got this far! We've got to try and keep MOON MAZE!' she said.

'That's right!' Belinda and Tracy agreed. 'Whatever it takes!'

Greg and Steffie smiled gratefully at them.

'Yes!' Steffie said. 'It's only for as long as it takes you to finish writing the game. After that, they just have to give in!'

'Well, you've changed!' he said, surprised.

Steffie nodded. 'I feel better now we've got some help,' she told him. 'Not so much in danger. In fact, I'm sure things are going to be all right!'

Holly looked at Greg. 'What do you say?' she asked.

He put a hand to his forehead and pressed his temple with his thumb and forefinger. He looked torn by doubt; tired and worried. 'I don't know. Maybe it's just too dangerous!' he said. 'They're closing in all the time!'

She nodded and held her breath. She could feel the air tingle with suspense and fear. 'We'll do what we can to help,' she promised quietly. 'Even if it means trying to move you away from here.'

Greg took a deep breath. 'I don't want to let them beat me!' he said. And after another short pause, he said, 'OK, I'll finish the disk! We'll prove we can do it and we'll wreck Megaware International!'

8 False alarm

Greg made his decision and Holly turned to an exhausted looking Steffie. 'Don't worry, we won't let you down. Do you want to join the three of us and sleep over at my place?'

Too tired to resist, Steffie agreed. 'I'm relieved more than anything, not to have to keep Greg secret from you any longer,' she said.

They were standing in the cluttered corridor, nervous now about having to take the route back down to school without being seen. Greg came up to Holly and spoke softly. 'Thanks a million,' he said. 'But remember, you'll all have to take great care!' His tone sent a chill down her spine. She opened the door a tiny crack and began the painstaking lookout for Sharon Hall's silver car.

The end of lesson bell rang just as the Mystery Club made it back to the fifth form centre. Lessons took over, and the tennis court was the next place they could get together. It was during their games lesson.

Belinda, who hated all energetic sports except riding, threw the ball up to serve, swung her racket and missed. The ball hit her foot and rolled sideways. Tracy picked it up. 'You'll never make it to Wimbledon,' she sighed.

Belinda laughed out loud. 'Thank heavens for that!' She tried again, but with the same result. 'Just think – all that training, all that coaching! A special high protein diet. Yuck!' she proclaimed. 'Life would be absolutely miserable!'

Tracy laughed too. 'Your problem is you have no ambition.' She threw the ball in the air and smashed it over the net. Then she trotted forward to collect more balls.

'That's not true!' Belinda contradicted. She winked at Holly. 'My ambition is to taste every single flavour of ice-cream in the world!'

Holly swung her racket in a practice backhand. 'And mine is to find a safe place to hide Greg Smith!' she said.

She hit the tennis ball with extra energy. It found the perfect place in the tramlines on the opposite side of the net. She looked up with narrowed eyes. 'A safe place for Greg Smith!' she repeated.

Tracy and Belinda came to join her in a huddle while the games teacher, Miss Wood, coached the group on the next court.

'Are you sure about moving him?' Tracy asked. 'It seems pretty risky to me!'

Holly nodded. 'It won't take Sharon and Tom Stone much longer to track him down. After all, *we* just managed to do it. I don't think we have much of a choice,' she said.

But Holly needed to check something with them both before they made a firm plan. 'Listen, things have moved pretty quickly lately. From guessing that Steffie was in some kind of trouble, we've gone on through kidnap to huge industrial theft and death threats!' She looked quickly and sharply at Belinda and Tracy. 'Say now if you don't want to go any further!'

Tracy glanced at Belinda. 'Are we a Mystery Club or not?' she demanded.

Miss Wood approached, ready to start them off in a game. She held up a set of balls. 'Come along, Tracy!' she called.

Belinda nodded firmly at Tracy and Holly. 'We stick together!' she said.

Holly smiled with relief. 'Great! Come on. Maybe it'll just be a case of keeping an eye on Steffie, moving Greg as quickly as possible, and getting them both safely through the next few days!' She left them and ran over to the other side of the net.

'Then he can finish writing the game,' Belinda agreed. She too had run the length of the court and was out of breath. 'I'm so unfit!' she wailed.

'Well here's a nice easy shot,' Tracy called. She

took up position opposite Belinda. 'So you're really sure we have to move him?' she said to Holly as she whacked the ball hard across the net at Belinda, who missed it.

'Listen!' Holly said. Belinda had gone off good-naturedly to retrieve the ball. 'We managed to track him down through Steffie, didn't we? Well honestly, it won't take Sharon and Tom much longer.'

Tracy nodded in agreement. She kept an eye on the high ball Belinda had just lobbed over the net.

'Maybe it'll be nice and easy. No great drama!' Holly reassured her. But she felt in her bones that this wasn't likely.

'Or maybe Sharon and Tom will take one last shot!' Tracy said with a grim expression and a deadly aim of the ball.

In the French lesson just before lunch, the Mystery Club began to plan ahead. 'If we have to move Greg . . .' Tracy said pointedly.

Holly nodded. 'We do!'

Tracy sighed. 'Well, if we do, just remember it's half-term vacation tomorrow. No kids around. It makes it pretty difficult to go round without anyone seeing us.'

Belinda agreed. 'It's certainly easier to smuggle someone out of a busy place. You can just mingle with the crowd.'

'Belinda, *qu'est-ce que vous dites*?' Madame Lavalle asked in an irritated voice. '*Taisez-vous, s'il vous plait!*'

'Sorry!' Belinda said. She tried to keep her head down and she managed to stay quiet for a full ten seconds. 'I think it would be better to get it over with today!' she said suddenly.

'Maybe.' Holly nodded and tried for a while to concentrate on French verbs. She knew only too well that the plan had to be a good one to convince Greg and Steffie that it was a risk worth taking. 'Let's think carefully before we act,' she said.

At lunch, Holly, Belinda and Tracy had just managed to settle with their sandwiches in Steffie's usual corner. They looked round anxiously, waiting for her to show up. 'There's a lot to talk about!' Holly said. She felt keyed up, with a horrible nervous feeling that Sharon Hall was round every corner and Tom Stone at the end of every corridor.

'Calm down!' Belinda advised. She was already well into her second sandwich. 'You're giving me indigestion.'

'That's impossible!' Holly joked. But her mind was still full of worries.

'OK then, you're giving *yourself* an ulcer,' Belinda pointed out. 'Don't worry, Steffie's bound to show up soon.'

114

'She's not worrying, are you, Holly?' Tracy said. 'This is called forward planning, thinking ahead, that's all!' She tried to lighten the mood, but she herself was tense with anxiety.

'Then why are you trying to open the wrong end of your orange juice carton?' Belinda pointed out to Tracy.

The dining-hall gradually filled with students. They queued, sat or lounged in corners. It was easy to miss someone in the crowd, but they knew Steffie always made her way over here.

'So we're going to suggest a place for Greg to hide when she finally shows up?' Tracy said.

'Yes, but where?' Holly had run through all the places she could think of; the Smiths' own house, a hotel in town, or somewhere much further away? All seemed fraught with danger, or else much too obvious to consider.

'Right!' Tracy nodded and fell silent.

The truth was, they were still working on it. Holly turned to Belinda for help.

Belinda shook her head. 'Sorry.' They sat nervously waiting. The heavy question hovered overhead: where to hide Greg Smith?

And then chaos struck. A bell began to ring throughout the school; five sharp rings, then a constant blast of sound.

'Fire!' someone yelled. 'That's the fire bell!'

Instantly the corridors were brimming with

pupils following arrows on the wall to the nearest escape point. The bell had shattered the routine of the school day. Everyone walked quickly, urgently towards the exits.

'Where's the fire?' Holly whispered to Belinda, who walked just in front of her with Tracy as they hurried out of the dining-hall.

'Search me!' Belinda said. 'Maybe it's a false alarm!' There was no smell of smoke, no flames.

But the fire-drill moved ahead, unstoppable. Pupils streamed from classrooms, and Holly lost sight of her two friends in the crush.

Then, just as she paused for breath by the drama room, she felt a rush of air. The door swung open, and a hand seized her by the arm! The hand pulled sharply and Holly fell sideways into the huge, blacked-out space.

Instantly Holly was afraid. This was no practical joke, she knew. No one would be stupid enough to fool around during a fire-drill! But she could only grope on hands and knees, unable to see a single thing. There was a whiff of perfume, a click of high heels on the polished wooden floor. Behind her, Holly could sense a heavier presence; someone moving forward in soft soled shoes, who wrenched her up on to her feet. 'Help!' Holly screamed against the jangling, deafening fire bell. Even then, she knew no one would hear.

'Go ahead, scream!' said a low, mocking voice.

In the gloom Holly began to make out glints of gold jewellery, and then Sharon Hall's made up, mask-like face took shape. It was smiling without humour, without any feeling whatsoever.

'It's OK, we won't hurt you,' the woman said. 'We just want you to tell us all you know about Steffie Smith and her precious brother.'

Holly didn't believe her. She felt Tom Stone's grip tighten and he was already hurting. His arm slid under hers from behind, and up round the back of her neck, so that her head was forced forward.

'And don't worry, we're not going to burn to death in the flames,' Sharon Hall promised. '*We* set off the alarm!' She smiled. 'We thought even Steffie would have to put in an appearance for a fire-drill – she's been proving elusive so far today!'

'Come on, let's move it!' Stone hissed. 'Let's get what we want and let's get out of here!'

'OK,' Sharon said calmly. 'Seeing you walking down the corridor was too good a chance to miss. So we grabbed you instead; almost as good as Steffie in the circumstances.'

Holly pictured the whole school assembled out on the tennis courts. They'd be lining up in neat rows, far from here, to be checked by the teachers. It would take a long time to register her as missing.

'What do you want me to tell you?' she asked. The pressure from Tom's grip grew, strong as a vice.

117

Sharon Hall's painted smile stretched wider. 'Well, first of all, let me make a small observation,' she said. 'We don't like nosey kids. We don't like kids who snoop and get in the way, and start playing detective, get it?'

Holly tried to nod, but her head was locked down, close to her chest. Her neck hurt, she could hardly breathe.

'OK, so now the big question,' Sharon Hall said smoothly. 'Where's Steffie Smith hiding that brother of hers, the computer whiz-kid? We want you to tell us.'

'I don't know!' Holly cried. She'd begun to feel dizzy. The pain in her neck almost made her faint.

'Sure you do. You're a smart kid,' Sharon Hall coaxed. 'We've been watching you!'

'Really, I don't know!' Holly cried again. How long could she hold out?

She felt a wave of fear wash over her. She remembered Greg's vain warning; 'Take great care!' She saw how difficult it was to try and hide anything from these two. Luck was on their side, and they were dangerously determined.

'We know you paid a visit to the Smith place,' Sharon said casually. 'And you certainly messed things up for us during our little day trip to London!'

Holly felt herself go cold all over. Tom kept his

118

grip tight round her neck. But it was Sharon's calm, cool voice that really frightened her. This woman would never lose control, would never give in. Holly struggled to raise her head so she could look her in the eye, but Tom kept it locked down in his painful hold.

Sharon arched a slim eyebrow. 'What we want to know is really very simple, very easy!' She put on a voice full of patience, like a nursery-school teacher trying to coax an answer out of a shy four year old. 'You see, all you have to do now is tell us where Steffie's big brother is hiding out! Not difficult, is it?' She looked at her watch. 'We have about two minutes to get the answer,' she said. She folded her arms placidly.

Holly was at her wits' end. The fire bell drilled into her with its harsh clanging. The building had emptied and she was left with an eerie, hollow feeling in the pit of her stomach.

'Well?' Sharon insisted.

Holly felt Tom force her head forward a fraction.

'I won't tell you!' she gasped. 'You can do what you like to me!' She would never give Greg away.

But then everything changed. In an instant, with a sudden blast of light flooding the dark drama room, the door burst open. Tom released his grip. Sharon spun round to see the intruder.

'Steffie!' Holly cried out. She recognised the slim,

determined figure and wrenched herself free from Tom Stone. She ran towards the door.

'This way, quick!' Steffie yelled. 'Follow me!'

Holly followed blindly. She headed for Steffie in the square of light beyond the blacked-out room. She heard Tom swear and his heavy footsteps set off in pursuit. Then he blundered against some heavy object. They heard him fall and swear, closed the door on him and Sharon, and left them in complete darkness.

They ran into the empty, echoing entrance hall, then darted down a side corridor into a small room tucked away out of sight. 'Quick, in here! They might not spot this place!' Steffie gasped.

They slipped inside the narrow door. It was a room used by the music and drama departments for storage; full of huge musical instruments and old props from past school productions. There were grey dustsheets everywhere covering bulky, shapeless objects. And there was a partly hidden spiral staircase going up out of sight. Breathless and terrified, Holly closed the door behind them.

'How did you find me?' she gasped. 'I really thought I'd had it back there!'

Steffie nodded grimly. 'I was trying to catch you up after the fire alarm went off. But you three shot off from the dining-hall and I was caught up with all the other kids filing out of school.' She pulled Holly further into the storeroom, away from the door. 'As a matter of fact, I've been busy keeping out of Sharon's way myself!'

Holly nodded. She began to look around the cluttered room for a place to hide. Out in the entrance hall, doors banged and Tom Stone's footsteps criss-crossed from drama room to office to music room. How long would it be before he found this little hidden doorway?

Steffie continued. 'I saw them cruising up and down the hill. I'm scared stiff they're going to move in on Greg. Anyway, when the alarm went, I was behind you in the corridor and I saw them grab you! It took me a couple of minutes to work out what to do. I mean, one second there you were following the fire-drill. Next second, gone!'

'It was terrible!' Holly said.

Steffie nodded gravely. 'So I nipped out of sight down here for a while. Just to let the building empty and think what to do next. I didn't exactly fancy barging in on Sharon and Tom. But in the end, what else was there to do?' She paused. 'They'd grabbed you and I couldn't waste time worrying what they'd do to me if they caught me!'

Holly closed her eyes and took a deep breath. 'Thanks!' she said. 'But listen, it's not going to take them long to find us. Sooner or later they're going to spot this little storeroom!'

Steffie nodded. 'But we have to stay put. We don't have any choice, do we?' They heard the doors opening and banging shut, and the footsteps running from room to room. 'We're trapped!'

'Maybe.' Holly cast an eye around the storeroom. 'Come on, we have to find a good place to hide!'

9 Murder in mind

There was no more time to talk. Quickly Holly and Steffie scanned the room. 'Up there?' Holly suggested. She pointed to the spiral stairs.

She leaped up the metal stairs two at a time, with Steffie hard on her heels. But the staircase led only to a platform, edged with an iron railing and about six metres square. It was piled with more musical instruments and old costumes.

'Where does it lead to?' Steffie urged from three or four steps below.

'Nowhere!' Holly gasped. 'We're stranded!'

But they heard the click of an opening door down below, and the renewed blare of the fire bell. Instantly they scrambled on to the platform.

'They found it!' Steffie gasped. 'Hide here, under this pile of curtains.' She began to burrow silently into their musty depths. Holly soon followed.

Tom Stone investigated below. They heard him lift the dustsheets and shift a few instruments. He cursed under his breath. They heard the click-click of Sharon Hall's heels follow him into the room. 'Slippery little customers!' she exclaimed, almost as if she was enjoying the chase. Holly could hear her voice, muffled by the pile of curtains, but half laughing at Tom's irritation. 'Don't worry, they can't have beamed themselves up off the planet!' she said. Her voice got nearer all the time. Then Holly heard her say, 'Hey, what's this?' And her accomplice came to join her at the foot of the metal stairway.

'No, they've not beamed themselves up off the planet,' he said. 'Just up to the top of these stairs, I guess,' There was a pause, then his footsteps began to climb.

'Hey!' Sharon called. He stopped. 'We're not talking kidnap this time!' Her voice sounded hard and determined. 'This time we use force, OK? One of them is bound to break!'

Holly shuddered, but it gave her an extra few seconds to think of an escape plan. She lifted one edge of the curtains and peered out.

'I'm out of patience,' Sharon told him icily. 'I want Greg Smith. And I want that disk!'

Again Holly shrank from the cold threat. Sharon Hall sounded as if she was talking to her hairdresser, not giving instructions to maim or murder. This was a woman completely without conscience.

Steffie seemed to have curled up and almost stopped breathing beside Holly. Then Sharon stopped

124

talking and Tom Stone continued up the steps towards them.

Holly grabbed hold of Steffie's arm. No way was she going to wait here any longer, to feel Tom's nasty stare gazing down on them in their hiding-place. And she thought she'd spotted one chance of escape; slim and dangerous, but possible!

'This way!' she hissed at Steffie.

'No!' Steffie resisted. 'There's no way out!

But Holly insisted. 'Yes there is a way! There's a pipe running along the walls up here. We can swing out on to it!' Already she was pushing off the heavy curtains. She dragged Steffie clear of them and tried to judge the strength of the brackets supporting the pipe. They were old-fashioned, heavy metal brackets and the pipe itself looked strong and solid. If they managed to swing on to it and along to the end of the wall, they would reach a window with a narrow opening section. 'Let's see if we can squeeze out of there! Come on, Steffie!' She pointed to the opening.

Her voice was frantic. Tom's footsteps had paused on the stairs again, but it was the ominous pause of someone who'd heard movement. Then he began to race up, two at a time. 'Got them!' he yelled back to Sharon.

Holly pushed Steffie over the rail of their plat-form and made her grip one of the strong brackets. Then she followed. It was high and dangerous out there. The pipe was half a metre from the ceiling and some five metres from the floor below. They moved forward by swinging and hauling themselves along to the next bracket, monkey fashion. Holly's arms ached with the strain, but they were clear of the platform. Tom Stone stood there, hands on hips. 'What the . . .!' he yelled.

'Keep moving!' Holly whispered. She glanced way down at the humped dustsheets and Sharon Hall staring up at them in amazement.

Steffie swung forward and grabbed the next bracket. Her legs bashed the wall. She was too terrified to look down.

'Well, go on, what are you waiting for?' Sharon asked. 'Follow them! Get them back!'

'You go get them!' Tom muttered. 'Those pipes won't take my weight!'

'Don't argue, just go ahead!' she shouted, almost angry, almost out of control.

So he leaned out and tested his weight on the pipe. He kept firm hold of the railing. The pipe creaked and shifted under his added weight.

Steffie screamed and Holly drew breath sharply. Smatterings of plaster broke loose and fell to the ground. The pipe shuddered. *It's going to break*! she thought. Her arms felt as if they'd been pulled from their sockets, but still they swung and edged forward towards the high window.

But Tom had decided to risk it. He heaved

himself across to the pipe and hung free of the platform. The pipe held fast. Gingerly at first, he began to edge after them.

'Oh God!' Steffie cried. 'He's going to bring the whole thing down!'

Holly felt her breath come fast and shallow. There was two metres of wall to manoeuvre along, then a corner, then the window. They had to reach that window!

But Tom Stone was fearless and athletic. He was gaining ground. Steffie panted and covered the distance painfully slowly. They heard Sharon shout encouragement from below.

They reached the corner. Tom could almost stretch forward to grab Holly. But he pushed himself a few centimetres too far, a second too fast. The wall brackets creaked, plaster cracked. He must have panicked. He didn't stop to think how to take the corner after Steffie and Holly. He swung forward. One hand missed the pipe and slipped. His weight fell sideways. He hung precariously from one hand.

'Watch out!' Sharon shouted.

Steffie closed her eyes and froze.

'Keep going!' Holly told her. They'd reached the open window.

Tom Stone hung on and managed to right himself. Like a gymnast, he hauled himself up with one arm and managed to catch hold of a bracket with the other. He was stable again. He clung to the pipe for a moment, catching his breath.

Steffie came back to life. Still Holly urged her on. 'Swing forward and grab the curtain rail. See if it will take your weight!' They had to be able to trust the heavy, old rail.

Steffie did as she was told and nodded. She swung one last time and slotted her legs into the opening. Then she began to wriggle through the window. Swiftly Holly followed. They'd made it so far!

They found themselves outside in the fresh air, comfortably standing on one of the wide stone ledges that decorated the Victorian frontage of the Winifred Bowen-Davies School. Holly glanced down and gasped with disbelief. She'd been prepared for another scary climb down to ground level, with Tom still in hot pursuit. But standing out on the ivy covered ledge, they found they had an audience!

'Steady on!' a man's voice called. 'Stay where you are! We'll go and get our ladders.'

And several firefighters in shiny yellow coats, who'd been checking every corner of the building for signs of fire, ran to their fire engines.

They came back with metal ladders and began to scale them.

'Great!' Holly said to Steffie with a sigh of relief and a wide grin. She greeted the firefighter with a smile and insisted on climbing down the ladder herself.

'Are you sure you're both OK?' he checked.

They nodded.

'Next time I suggest you use the door like everyone else!' he said. He guarded Holly and Steffie every inch of the way down.

'We would, but it's a long story!' Holly gasped. She could have cried with relief to have her feet on solid ground again. 'Let's just say we were trapped in there,' she explained.

'And if you go inside that storeroom you'll find the reason!' Steffie gabbled.

A couple of firefighters went hurrying off through the main door to investigate. But they came back within minutes, shaking their heads. 'Nothing in there.' they said, puzzled, and walked back to their fire engine.

Holly stared at Steffie. 'Sharon must have seen all the activity with the ladders from inside the room. She must have called Stone to come down from the pipe.'

Steffie nodded. 'Yes and I suppose then they made their usual quick getaway.'

Holly smiled. 'I bet she's kicking herself for raising that alarm in the first place!' she whispered.

'Now that the fire service has stopped her getting at us!'

Holly grew serious again. 'But it doesn't actually solve our problem.'

'No, they'll still be on our backs,' Steffie agreed. 'Listen, Holly, tell me the truth. What do you think Greg's chances are of hanging on to MOON MAZE?

Holly thought long and hard. 'I don't know. Getting hold of that game is the only thing Sharon Hall cares about. She hates Greg, and Megaware can't afford to let him score another success after SPACE WALK.' She felt a small shudder go through her. 'Honestly, Steffie, I don't know what Greg's chances are!'

At last the fire service gave the school the all-clear and things returned to normal.

Belinda and Tracy came racing up from the tennis courts as soon as the teachers dismissed them back into lessons. Holly saw them come charging up the steps, round the front of the school.

'What happened?' Belinda gasped. Her hair blew untidily across her face and she was red with the effort of running up steps, but she'd kept pace with Tracy. 'We were really worried about you!'

Holly described their great escape. 'My main worry was whether that pipe would take all our weight!' she exclaimed. 'I had visions of the whole thing coming crashing down!'

Tracy gave a low whistle. 'Are you sure you're

OK?' she said. 'We can't afford to lose you right now!'

Holly and Steffie nodded.

'I'm just glad it wasn't me,' Belinda said. 'I can't stand heights.' She pushed her hair behind her ears. 'You know, for a kids' game, MOON MAZE is proving to be pretty risky business!' she said, shaking her head.

Everyone straggled back into school for afternoon lessons. There was a ragged atmosphere of broken routine and anticlimax. Steffie said she'd have to go, else she'd be in trouble. 'Again!' she grinned.

'Is it safe to go to lessons?' Tracy asked. 'I mean, it seems like, it's getting to the point where they'll do absolutely anything to find Greg!' Her normally bright face looked deadly concerned and serious.

Holly listened. 'Look, I think we may have a bit of breathing space,' she said. 'Sharon and Tom will probably lie low while things get back to normal this afternoon.' She turned to Steffie just as they were about to go their separate ways. 'We know for sure we can't go and bother Miss Horswell about this again,' she told her. 'So that's out.'

Steffie agreed. 'School used to be such a simple, straightforward old place!' she sighed.

'And safe!' Holly added.

Steffie raised her eyebrows. 'I know. I'm sorry, Holly!'

'Don't be!' Holly looked round at Tracy and Belinda. 'The Mystery Club said we'd help, didn't we?'

'Oh sure!' Tracy laughed. 'Just don't make me walk down a corridor by myself, that's all!' She looked with exaggerated caution to left and right as they walked.

'I don't know about anything else, but I do know I'd like my lunch!' Belinda complained. 'And I just missed it!' She thought of her sandwiches, half-eaten, lying on the dining-hall table, and her unopened packet of chocolate biscuits.

Holly laughed. 'Meet at afternoon break?' she suggested.

The others agreed.

'By the bike shed?' Belinda asked.

They all looked to Steffie to see if that was OK. She nodded, but when she spoke her tone was grave. 'You know, I don't think Greg is safe where he is for much longer!' Tears came to her eyes as she admitted it.

'That's just what we were saying earlier,' Belinda told her softly.

Steffie sighed. 'But I can't for the life of me think where we can move him to!' She seemed to turn to Holly again and appeal to her.

'Don't worry!' Holly said. She tried to sound more confident than she felt. 'At least we all agree now that we have to move him!'

'It's going to be hard, but if we leave him here any longer, we might as well just hand MOON MAZE over to them,' Tracy said. 'They know he's here somewhere!'

They nodded silently and went their separate ways. Holly put her head down and hurried down the corridor to her English lesson. How could they get a grown man out of the school grounds with those two watching like hawks? Take them by surprise? Do the unexpected?

She thought hard all through the lesson. Then, right at the end, just as she handed in her dog-eared copy of the play they were reading, a small idea shone like a light in a dark attic. Holly packed her bag and shot out of the room. It was time for their rendezvous. 'Maybe! Just maybe!' she thought.

10 Hijack!

'This is all very well,' Tracy pointed out. The four of them sat on a low wall behind the bike shed. 'But here we are making plans without even asking Greg! Shouldn't we include him in whatever we decide?'

'Shh!' Belinda warned. She glanced behind into a long garden of a big house that backed on to the school grounds. It was empty. 'We can't be too careful,' she said.

'I agree.' Holly nodded slowly.

Only Steffie stayed silent. She looked worn out with worry.

'Hey!' Tracy announced, with a sudden gleam in her blue eyes. 'I've got an idea.'

'Uh-oh,' Belinda said, shaking her head. 'Here comes trouble.'

'Come on, what's the idea?' Holly asked, shifting closer to Tracy.

'Well, we need to talk with Greg one more time before we stage this grand escape plan,' Tracy said eagerly. She took a deep breath. 'Why don't you and Steffie sneak up there now?' She paused.

'And . . .?' Holly urged.

'And why don't Belinda and I make ourselves into deliberate decoys? You know, we set it up as if we're going to lead these Megaware creeps straight to Greg and the precious disk! They follow us, and you two sneak off to the old caretaker's house!'

'Shh!' Belinda said again. They were surrounded by dark corners, bushes and trees where Tom and Sharon could be hiding.

Holly considered the plan. 'You think they're actually keeping watch now?' she asked. They talked in low, urgent whispers.

'Sure they are! Why would they let up? They think they've got you and Steffie cornered.'

They turned and peered at the leaves rustling in the garden behind. Was it the wind? Or was it Tom Stone creeping nearer to hear what they said?

'And how will we get them to follow you two instead of us?' Holly asked.

'OK, you want to see how?' Tracy demanded. She leaped up, ready for action.

Mystified, Holly turned to Steffie. 'What do you think?' she asked.

Steffie's pale, troubled face turned to each of them. 'I trust you three,' she said. 'And I'm past knowing what's best for Greg. Somehow I can't get myself to make decisions about it any more!'

135

Holly nodded and squeezed her hand. 'It's OK, don't worry.' Then she faced Tracy again. 'We haven't much time. What do you want us to do?'

'Improvise!' Tracy whispered. 'Just follow on from what I say and do. I'm about to start a great big argument with you, OK? And you and Steffie have to storm off inside saying you don't want to get involved.' She drew Belinda close to her. 'And you have to pretend to try and stop me, and run after me!'

Holly, Steffie and Belinda nodded. Holly knew there was no stopping Tracy now. 'Just take care!' she warned.

Tracy nodded, then she began. She turned on them, hands on hips. She began to argue. 'What do you mean, it's getting too risky?' she demanded. 'You've lost your nerve all of a sudden!'

Holly had to check an urge to grin. Tracy was a terrific actress. She looked genuinely fired up. Holly stood up to have her own say. 'I'm telling you, I'm sick of this! It's too dangerous! I'm not going to risk my neck any more!' She raised her voice and stared Tracy in the face.

Tracy tossed her head and strode a couple of steps up the slope, past the rows of bikes. 'We can't just dump him now!' she yelled. 'Just because things are getting a little tough!'

'Who says we can't?' Holly retorted. She was beginning to get into the part. 'I can go right now to Miss Horswell's office and tell her everything! I'm telling you, I don't want to be involved any longer!'

Steffie's eyes widened. She put out a hand to restrain Holly.

Belinda jumped off the wall and went to join Tracy. 'If you do that, we'll go straight to Greg's hotel room and warn him!' she declared. 'Right now! This instant!' She looked fiercely at Holly.

'Please yourself!' Holly yelled. She took one quick look up and down the bike-shed slope, then back into the long, empty garden. For the first time she was wishing desperately for a glimpse of Tom and Sharon. But if they were there at all, they were well hidden. 'You can go off to The Moorlands if you like! But I've had enough! I'm going straight to the Head!'

And she stormed off, back inside the building, chased by an anxious looking Steffie. They stepped through the door, then darted sideways and pressed themselves against the wall, out of sight. They waited and watched.

'Come on, Belinda!' she heard Tracy announce, still out by the bikes. 'Let's go and warn Greg right now!'

And before she'd got the words out of her mouth, she was racing up the slope followed by a dogged looking Belinda.

Holly kept watch. The two of them were up on

the main drive and still no shadowy figure emerged from the garden to jump the low wall and creep after Tracy and Belinda. Holly bit back her disappointment. Had Tracy overestimated Tom and Sharon? They were nowhere to be seen. Still she kept her fingers crossed and kept close watch.

Then a bike swayed against its neighbour on the rack. Holly heard the click of metal. She focused on the gloom of the bike shed. Someone climbed out from behind the rack and looked furtively all around. It was Tom Stone!

He turned to help Sharon climb clear of the bikes. Holly saw him talking urgently. She opened the door a fraction wider to hear what was said.

'OK, OK!' Sharon muttered. She straightened herself out. 'No panic!'

Tracy and Belinda had already reached the end of the drive. They'd slowed down, but they were heading out of school grounds.

Again Holly's heart sank. Tom and Sharon had overheard the fake argument, but they hadn't fallen for the decoy. Tracy's plan had failed.

'Come on, what are we waiting for?' Tom Stone urged.

Holly's hopes surged again.

'I said, no panic!' Sharon's calm, smooth voice insisted. 'You heard what the kid said. She said The Moorlands. That's the big hotel right opposite!'

Holly saw her smile and set off calmly up the

side of the school. Tom Stone managed to curb his impatience and walk alongside.

'So that's where sister Steffie has been sneaking off to every day!' Sharon's voice receded up the hill. 'And that's where big brother Greg has been holed up!' She laughed. 'Didn't I say it was somewhere really close to the school? And now these two kids are leading us right to him!'

Holly waited until she was sure they'd followed Belinda and Tracy right out of the gate. She craned around the door and watched them disappear from sight. Then she turned to Steffie. 'Brilliant!' she said. 'It worked!'

'Tracy's a genius!' Steffie agreed. A smile had come back to her drawn face.

But there was no time to celebrate. They had to go talk to Greg!

'Ready?' Holly asked Steffie. 'I'll follow you.' They checked to make sure that Tom and Sharon were well out of sight. Even so, Holly's heart beat fast as she ran.

Out on the main road, Tracy and Belinda had slowed right down.

'Any sign of them?' Tracy said for what felt like the hundredth time.

Belinda glanced back, hoping for a glimpse of Sharon and Tom. She saw the empty school drive, the slope running down past the overgrown hedge and the caretaker's old house where Greg was hidden. Beyond that was the huge grey outline of the school itself. 'Nothing,' she reported. Then suddenly she spotted a movement. 'Yes!' she said. 'I think it's them!'

Tracy grabbed Belinda's arm. She'd seen them too, walking quickly up towards the school gate away from school. 'Great!' She grinned. 'Bet you never thought you'd be glad to see those two!'

'Look as if we're still watching out for their car or something. Pretend we haven't seen them!' Belinda said.

They looked cautiously up and down the hill, then crossed the road, holding their breath. They made a beeline for the hotel grounds, straight in through the wide gateway, and marched up the drive to the grand glass entrance.

'What now?' Belinda gasped. She could see a receptionist sitting at her desk in the middle of an expanse of red and gold carpet. The woman seemed not to have seen them as they approached the door.

'We look for somewhere to hide!' Tracy muttered.

'Where?'

'In there!' Tracy pointed to some large laurel bushes growing to one side of the hotel's main entrance. 'When no one's looking, OK?'

Belinda nodded. She was ready. At the last

moment, as they approached the door, they leaped sideways into the deep cover of the bushes. 'Fingers crossed!' Belinda breathed.

They didn't have to wait long to see if they'd managed to draw Sharon and Tom all the way up here, away from school. The two of them had followed them up the hotel drive, looking up at the ivy-covered hotel and glancing at the name, 'The Moorlands', written in large gold letters above the door. 'You go ahead,' Tom told Sharon. 'I'll wait here.' He held the door open wide.

So Sharon went quickly and confidently up to the receptionist while Tracy and Belinda stayed safe in their hiding-place. They could glimpse Tom's face; the narrowed eyes and gritted teeth. They even heard the high, puzzled sound of the receptionist's voice as Sharon quizzed her.

'What happened?' Tom asked as she arrived back on the front step.

Sharon's face was flushed with anger. 'There's no one by the name of Greg Smith staying here!' she spat out.

In the laurel bushes, Tracy grinned at Belinda.

'Or anyone even remotely like him who's checked in under a different name!' Sharon went on. 'I described him to the woman at the desk. He's definitely not here!'

Tom Stone grunted. 'Looks like they tricked us.'

He cleared his throat and looked down to check some mud on his shoes.

'They sent us on a wild goose chase!' She looked angrily at Tom. 'And like idiots we fell for it.' She led the way back down the drive in a terrible temper.

Belinda could hardly wait until they were out of earshot. 'Brilliant!' she grinned. 'That's given Holly and Steffie plenty of time to go and see Greg!'

Tracy stood up and heaved a sigh of relief. 'But we've still got a long way to go!'

The smell of paint hit Holly again as they safely entered Greg's hiding-place. It was damp and gloomy as before. Steffie had tapped out a small rhythm on the door and Greg had opened it. Holly thought he looked tired and nervous, though he tried to hide it for Steffie's sake. 'Hi!' he greeted them. 'Welcome back to the ideal home!' He led them down the passage into what must have been the caretaker's kitchen. 'Running water,' he said. 'But no gas!'

'You should complain to the management!' Steffie said, more her old, brisk self again. She handed him a food parcel from her pocket and sat up on the old draining-board. 'You've no idea what we've just been through to get here!'

Greg looked narrowly at Holly. 'Why do I get the idea that this isn't just a casual visit?' he joked.

'Good guess!' she said brightly. Then she decided to jump in with both feet. 'We want to move you!' she said. 'It's getting too dangerous here. The idea is to move you out in secret. The problem is, where to? I've been working it all out during my English lesson.' She paused before she delivered her flash of inspiration. 'You can come to my house!'

'Just like that?' Greg put his hands in his pockets. He rested back against a wall cupboard. 'Won't your parents mind?'

Holly quickly explained the situation. 'The house is empty at the moment because my parents are away for a couple of days. I've arranged for Belinda and Tracy to stay over. There'll be no one else there besides us. It's the safest place I can think of!' She turned to Steffie for approval. 'What do you think?'

Steffie thought for a moment. 'It sounds good. If you're sure you want to?'

Greg considered it too. 'I think you're right,' he said. 'This seemed like a good place to hide until Sharon got back on my trail and made life a misery for everyone.' He paused. 'And I don't need much longer to finish the disk; another day or so.'

'But I don't think you'll get away with even one more night here,' Holly said.

'They're close behind us all the time,' Steffie said. She told him about the narrow escape in the drama room and Tracy's brilliant decoy.

143

'That settles it!' Greg stood up straight and came across to Holly. 'We've got to clear out of here, and your place sounds good.' He paused. 'But getting out of here is still the real problem.' He paced up and down, coming to a halt by the narrow, grimy kitchen window. He stared out.

Holly looked at Steffie. How *did* you get a grown man out of a house in a place that was being watched round the clock?

Suddenly Greg turned back towards them. 'I've got it!' he said.

When he grinned, he looked younger than twenty-two; just like a kid, Holly thought. She and Steffie answered his beckoning hand.

'Come over here!' he whispered. 'See that school minibus of yours?'

Peering over his shoulder on tiptoe, Holly could just see the top of the white Winifred Bowen-Davies minibus parked in its usual place to one side of the main entrance. It was old and rickety, with the school crest emblazoned on its sides. It was used for games matches and educational trips. 'Yes,' she said. 'I see it.'

'Well, we're going to use that,' Greg said calmly.

'Just like that?' Holly said.

'What?' Steffie nearly fell backwards. 'Use that old thing? It wouldn't go more than fifty kilometres an hour!'

'No, hang on; I think it could work!' Holly said more slowly. 'If only because it's so totally unexpected!'

'Thanks,' Greg said. 'No one would suspect us. Sharon Hall won't look twice at the old school minibus taking a group of girls off to a tennis match or something!'

'Especially right after the end of school,' Holly joined in. 'With everyone pouring out of the place at once! You and I, Tracy and Belinda will get dressed up in our games kit. We'll look just like a normal team!' she paused. 'But what about keys to the minibus?'

Greg nodded. 'I know, that's another problem. Where are they kept?'

Holly's hopes faded. 'In the office. The secretary guards them with her life!'

But Steffie was gradually entering into the plan. 'The key is a problem,' she said thoughtfully. 'But today's the day a few sixth formers would usually volunteer to clean out the minibus. I can go up and ask for the key as part of the clean-up group. The secretary wouldn't suspect a thing!'

'Perfect!' Greg signalled them to wait a second and slipped out of the room.

'I think this is going to work!' Holly said. Her hopes had revived since Tracy's decoy had turned out so well, and now they were beginning to soar.

Greg soon came back, transformed from the smooth young executive into an old school caretaker! A tatty brown cotton overall and a flat cap had made him unrecognisable. He carried an old black hold-all containing the computer and his precious disk.

'What do you think of my disguise?' he said.

Holly and Steffie had to smother their laughter.

'You look perfect for the part!' Steffie giggled.

'I remembered they'd just been left hanging behind a cupboard door,' he explained. He pulled the cap down over his forehead. 'Do you think we'll get away with it?'

'Yes!' they both said.

'Good!' He took off the cap and stuffed it in a pocket.

'Meet us by the minibus at four o'clock!' Holly said. 'We'll be all ready in our games kit. Steffie will have the key.'

'Wait until you see us all before you set off from here,' Steffie warned. 'Then we can make a quick getaway!'

Greg showed them to the door. 'Don't worry, I'll take all responsibility for the minibus.' he said. 'If we ever get out of here in one piece, that is!'

The girls nodded and headed back to school. Greg's last words echoed uneasily in their heads.

Steffie, Holly, Tracy and Belinda changed into their

146

games outfits as soon as the final bell released them from lessons. No one spoke as they laced up their tennis shoes and took their rackets from their lockers. And no one else noticed anything unusual about four girls meeting up at the front entrance, waiting to be driven off to a tennis match.

'Have a good half-term!' people called as they poured out of the building in all directions.

Holly and the others nodded, too nervous to say anything. They waited as Steffie went to the office for the key. She came back nodding and holding it up in her right hand. 'It worked!' she whispered. So they all went out into the full sunlight, hoping and praying.

'The things I do for the Mystery Club!' Belinda groaned. 'Standing out in the hot sun, pretending to be keen on games!'

Teachers criss-crossed the playground and the drive, carrying heavy loads of books up to their cars. They drove off without a second glance at the patiently waiting tennis team. Even Miss Earnshaw wished them good luck for their match as she headed for home.

'Where is he?' Steffie whispered anxiously. 'He must have seen us by now!'

'Here he is, he's coming!' Holly spotted him first.

'Where?' Belinda and Tracy asked.

'There, in the brown overall!' Holly pointed

to the new caretaker coming towards them, cap down, old black hold-all in one hand.

Tracy and Belinda hadn't recovered from the shock of his disguise before Greg had arrived, taken the keys from Steffie, unlocked the back door of the minibus and told them to climb in quick!

Within a few more seconds, he'd opened the driver's door, hopped in and started the engine.

It spluttered and whined. Finally it choked into life. 'Thank heavens we didn't bump into any of the games teachers!' Holly breathed.

Greg backed the bus on to the drive, then eased into first gear. There was hardly a curious glance from all the hundreds of pupils on their way out of school as the minibus made its way to the gate. This was working like a dream, Holly thought.

But the main road was busy and partly blocked by parents waiting to collect their children. Greg braked and tapped impatiently on the steering wheel. 'Come on!' he muttered.

In the back, Holly tensed up. They needed to be away from here before Sharon and Tom got a chance to close in and take a look. She peered through the window, anxiously scanning the road for the silver car.

At last, Greg saw a gap and could ease out into the traffic.

'Go left up the hill!' Holly said. 'We'll take a back route; less traffic!' She gripped the metal bar behind

148

the driver's seat. 'It means taking a roundabout route out of town and then back.'

Greg nodded and crunched into bottom gear. They were on their way, up the hill in a rickety old minibus! The engine strained, the gears crashed. 'Not exactly inconspicuous, are we?' Greg muttered. He pulled the cap further over his face and hunched his shoulders.

'Once we're over the cattle grid up on to the moor we should be OK,' Holly promised. 'Everyone will have turned off by then.'

He nodded. All the girls kept watch. So far there was no sign of Sharon Hall. The minibus droned on up the slope.

As it came to more level ground, with heather stretching to right and left of the road, Holly thought she caught a glimpse of a car cruising way down a side road to the left, in an estate of new houses. Her heart sank. But a second look proved it wasn't the same car. She told Greg to get a move on, just in case. The minibus clattered over a metal cattle grid.

'Successful operation!' Greg said triumphantly. He threw off the cap, patted the black hold-all and looked back at them.

But Holly scrunched round and looked back down the hill. A car was coming out of that side road. It was silver and it was following them! She gasped. 'Greg, look in your mirror!'

The car was still small in the distance, but gaining fast. Greg looked and nodded. 'It's them!' he said grimly.

The girls gripped the seats as Greg put his foot down hard on the accelerator. The bus swung round a bend with a squeal of brakes. Then another swerve. They swayed from side to side.

'Quickly, they're catching up!' Holly cried.

'Stop, it's hopeless!' Steffie said. 'I knew we'd never make it!'

Holly stared at her. 'We can't give up now! Turn right!' She knew this road a lot better than Sharon and Tom. 'Down this side track; go on!'

Greg swung the minibus on to the rough track, just below the tall horseshoe of rocks known as High Almscliff. There was heather carpeting the rocky landscape as far as the eye could see.

'I think they saw us!' Tracy moaned.

They clung on grimly. 'Keep going!' Holly shouted. Dust rose, gravel crunched and shot up from the loose surface. 'Don't stop!'

The silver car overshot the half-hidden turning. It squealed to a halt, reversed, and found the lane at last.

'We gained a few seconds!' Holly said. 'Keep going!'

Greg urged the old minibus down the farm road. 'It's only a matter of time before they catch us,' he said in a low voice.

'No, we may be in luck!' Holly shot to her feet and was hanging on to a rail beside Greg's seat. 'Look!'

In a field just to the left, a herd of black and white cows lumbered towards a gate. A boy in a red checked jacket was opening the gate from the field into the lane. Holly sprang to the window, lowered it and shouted frantically. 'Let us through!' she yelled as the minibus approached at breakneck speed. 'Please let us through!'

The cows trundled mildly forward, shoving at the gate. The boy looked puzzled. For a vital few seconds he held the gate fast.

Greg shot downhill, raising dust, rattling by.

'Thanks!' Holly yelled. 'You saved our lives!' She hung out of the window and waved madly at him as they passed.

The boy looked nonplussed, but he nodded and opened the gate to let the herd out across the lane into the farmyard opposite. Holly collapsed back in her seat. Through Greg's mirror, she saw the silver car slide to a halt on the far side of the black and white cows. Tom Stone leaped out to yell at the boy. It made no difference; they'd got clean away!

Greg kept his foot firmly on the accelerator. They sped out of sight of the cows, the farm, the car.

Holly gave directions, concentrating on the narrow road ahead. 'We're heading back into town now,' she promised.

Belinda kept a look out through the back window. 'Still no sign of them!' she reported. She bounced and jolted on the back seat. But she looked as if she'd begun to enjoy every moment.

'Nearly there!' Holly breathed. She'd zigzagged across country down lanes hardly anyone knew. The road behind them was empty. The town came into view, and her own house, tucked away up a lane where the old and new houses met. Her own sleepy, cosy house with no one around!

'Turn left!' Holly said at last to Greg. 'Down this drive. We're here!' She sighed happily as the minibus squeezed down the drive.

Holly could feel the relief as they all tumbled out. She went to open the garage doors and directed Greg carefully inside. The bus cleared the entrance and rolled slowly forward. It was hidden from view!

She closed the garage doors and breathed in deeply; the smell of cut grass, the feel of the sun on her face.

One more victory for Greg and Steffie! Holly led them quickly into the house past her father's empty workshop.

11   Lights in the lane

Holly went to rummage in her wardrobe for a quick change of clothes for everyone. The girls were downstairs making coffee and watching TV as if nothing had happened and this was a normal afternoon. But they needed to change out of their games kit.

She dug out T-shirts and trousers and laid them out on the bed. Her room looked just as it always did; the soft carpet, the pretty flowered wallpaper, the full-length, antique pine mirror. She sighed again and went downstairs.

'Pass me that magazine!' Belinda said. She had her feet up and a chocolate bar in one hand. 'Let's see what's on TV!'

Tracy dropped the magazine in her lap. 'I'm just going to ring home,' she said. 'I'd better check with my mum that she's remembered about me staying over. It should be OK.' She ambled out of the sitting-room into the kitchen.

Holly told Steffie that there were clean clothes up in her room. 'Thanks, Holly. It'll be good to get out of this tennis kit.' Steffie paused as she passed Holly, her blue eyes soft and warm. 'I just want to say how much we both appreciate all this!' she said. 'It was only your quick thinking that saved us out there this afternoon! Greg and I think you're all fantastic!'

Holly smiled and nodded. 'Well, we couldn't let them catch us!' she said. 'Even if we were only in a beaten up old minibus!'

They laughed at the memory of the herd of dozy dairy cows getting the better of Sharon Hall.

'Greg's making plans,' Steffie told her as she went upstairs. 'Go and see what you think.'

Greg was standing by the door to the garden, taking in the peace and quiet. Holly had already given him some of her father's casual clothes, and after a shower he was looking relaxed and fresh. Half in sunlight, half in shadow, he was beginning to look more like his old self; easy-going and strikingly handsome.

He turned to Holly and spoke his thoughts out loud. 'I think I'll work through the night to finish MOON MAZE. Then I'll hand it over to Nick and get it off my hands. After that we're home and dry!'

Holly listened. 'OK, you can work over in my dad's workshop,' she suggested. 'There's a desk and everything you need.'

Greg took the slim blue disk from his top pocket

154

and held it up. 'Just one more night! Then Nick copies this master disk and it's all systems go!' Greg paused and stared out into the garden. 'Even Sharon Hall isn't invincible in the end!' He turned to Holly. 'You know, I'd really like to see her face when MOON MAZE finally hits the shops.'

He contemplated the scene for a few moments, then brought himself back to the present. 'Is it OK if I use the phone?' he asked. 'I need to ring Nick to see if he can come here to pick up the finished disk in the morning.'

Holly nodded and went off satisfied with the part they'd played; with their neat escape plan and the way it had worked, with Greg's prospects for success in beating Megaware, and with the fantastic Mystery Club!

She looked in on Steffie, Tracy and Belinda. 'You know something; I think Greg's chances of hanging on to MOON MAZE have really improved!' she said.

Steffie smiled back.

'Say, do you have any ice-cream?' Tracy asked, as she wandered into the kitchen. She had a wide grin on her face. 'I just thought I'd better get in here quick before Belinda eats it all!'

Holly laughed. 'Time to celebrate?' she said.

Greg was soon ready to go out into Mr Adams's workshop to carry on working on the disk.

Holly showed him the way, reaching it by leaving the house by the front door and cutting diagonally across the cobbled yard, beyond the garage to a building that had once been a large garden shed. Now it was converted into a workspace for Holly's father, full of timber and woodworking tools, all neatly hung and stacked. Holly loved the smell of sawdust and resin in here, and the cosy corner her father had made for himself; a raised platform with a sofa, a reading lamp and a desk.

'Are you sure you'll manage OK in here?' she asked.

Greg had brought his computer and a sleeping-bag in case he grew too tired to work. He went over to the sofa, tested it for softness, then glanced all around. 'It's great!' he said. 'Can I pull down the blinds so no one can look in?'

Holly showed him how. 'Do you need anything else?' she asked.

He shook his head. 'No, it's the lap of luxury already!' he told her. 'After the nights with the paint tins and the broken furniture.' He studied the work Mr Adams was doing; the finished nest of tables, some unfinished bookcases. 'He must be proud of his work,' he said.

Holly nodded. 'He says the move up to Willow Dale was the best thing he ever did!' She ran her fingertips along the smooth surface of the bookcase. Then she said a quiet goodnight.

Greg smiled. 'Goodnight,' he said. He came to the door with her. 'And Holly, thanks!' he said.

It came from the heart. Holly smiled and went back to the house, filled with a warm glow.

'The question is,' Belinda was saying as Holly went into the kitchen. The girls were gathered round the table over the remains of the ice-cream. 'Do we need to set up a watch tonight while Greg works? Or do you think that's a bit over the top?'

'You mean, two of us should sleep, two stay awake to keep an eye on the workshop?' Steffie asked.

Belinda nodded. 'I'm just wondering if it's something we need to do as a precaution.'

'Oh, who'd find Greg here?' Tracy exclaimed. 'The minibus is hidden from view, and Sharon and Tom didn't know where we were heading.' She chewed an apple. 'They wouldn't dream of looking for him here!'

Holly agreed; it was unlikely. 'Still, I suppose we could make double sure,' she said. 'What harm would it do?'

So Tracy and Belinda agreed to take the first shift between eleven and one in the morning. Steffie and Holly would keep watch from one to three, and so on, in alternating shifts.

'It's just a question of sitting up by an upstairs window,' Holly explained. 'We can use Jamie's room. It has the best lookout position.'

157

She took them upstairs to her brother's room. 'There's only one way anyone can come up to the house by car, up the lane there. It's a dead end, so hardly anyone comes up here. We're bound to be able to check up on any strange cars we see.'

Tracy fiddled with Jamie's computer keyboard. By chance, SPACE WALK came up on screen. She began to play. They watched as Tracy's spaceman met alien spaceships and tried to zap his way past them.

'Uh-oh!' Tracy groaned. Her spaceman had just been zapped by a meteor. She began again.

After a few more aliens and meteors, Belinda looked up and asked, 'So how do we know if this car is "strange", should we happen to see one?'

Holly looked at her watch. It was ten-thirty. Outside it was already dark and quiet. 'Anything that comes down the lane at this time of night is strange!' she said. 'This is a very quiet part of town.'

'Hey, I zapped an alien!' Tracy exclaimed. 'And another! Oops!' Her spaceman came up against a new enemy.

Holly grinned at Belinda. 'I'll leave her to you! I'm off to bed. Wrap yourselves in these if it's cold.' She offered Belinda two sleeping-bags. 'And remember, wake Steffie and me at one!'

Belinda settled down with a yawn into Jamie's window seat. 'Don't worry, we will!' she said.

*   *   *

At one o'clock, Holly and Steffie crawled out of bed as Belinda and Tracy crawled in.

'Seen anything?' Holly mumbled. She rubbed the sleep out of her eyes, and pulled on some trousers and a sweater.

'Not a thing!' Tracy said, still yawning. 'Quiet as the grave! Wake us up at three!'

Belinda groaned from beneath the covers. 'This is some fun night Holly,' she complained. 'Spending half the night looking out of a window! She turned to the wall and fell instantly asleep.

Steffie followed Holly slowly along to Jamie's room. They wrapped sleeping-bags round their shoulders like fat giant shawls, then positioned themselves at the window.

From her side, Holly could see the yard and workshop to the right, and a glimpse of the lane to the left. It was all quiet. There was one low light on in the workshop, dulled by the closed blinds. Otherwise, the whole scene was dark.

The minutes ticked by. Red figures on Jamie's digital clock flicked slowly from 1:30 to 1:45. Holly's head began to nod gently forward. Out there was a vast, dark, empty space, except for a ghostly white shape which winged its way silently across the sky.

Holly's head shot up. It was an owl; that was all! An old barn owl. She glanced at Steffie and wondered whether to prop her back against the

159

wall, or to leave her where she was, half-slumped, half-asleep. She bent forward to help, but a low, white light outside caught her eye. She looked out of the window, down the lane to the main road beyond.

It was a sweep of headlights. The rays dipped and rose with the road. They turned down the lane and came nearer. Then they cut out. Once again there was complete darkness and silence.

Holly struggled free of her sleeping-bag. Steffie sighed, shifted, then sat bolt upright. 'Holly, what is it?' she whispered.

'A car, heading this way! I'm going to take look!' Swiftly she reached the bedroom door, aware of Steffie rushing along to catch her. She ran out on to the landing, sure-footed in the dark.

'Shouldn't we tell the others?' Steffie gasped. She had to grope along the banisters as they went down.

'No time,' Holly said. Let's take a look first!'

Who could this be, driving down their lane in the middle of the night? It could be innocent, she told herself. A romantic couple, someone lost. She crept to the front door, opened it, and felt the cool night air strike her face.

'Wait for me!' Steffie whispered. 'Where are you going?'

'Down the lane to check,' Holly said. She ran along the hard road surface, following the white line to see her way ahead. Steffie followed. They ran fifty metres, and stopped dead.

There was the car. It was low and gleaming, blocking the road. Its passenger door stood slightly open. In the moonlight it shone an eerie silver.

Holly lurched towards it and peered inside. It was empty. She looked at Steffie, aghast. 'Come on!' she whispered. They sprinted back up the lane, feeling the cold air in their throats, feeling their lungs begin to ache.

Holly led the way up her drive into the yard. The house was dark, but the light in the workshop was still on. She held up one hand. They stopped, waited and listened.

Something moved inside the workshop. The yard was dark and still. But again, something heavy scraped the floor. There was a thud, followed by a loud toppling and crashing of wood.

Steffie groaned. Holly gripped her by the wrist and ran forward. 'Come on!' she cried again. Together they crossed the yard.

The workshop door hung slightly ajar. Inside, everything had gone quiet. Instead of thuds and crashes, silence greeted them.

'Holly!' Steffie whispered. 'Be careful!'

Holly swallowed hard and pushed the door fully open. The yellow lamplight showed her father's neat stacks of wood collapsed and scattered over

161

the floor. She stepped inside, feeling sick with fear. His bookcase was upended at an angle. Everywhere was a mess!

'Greg!'

Steffie's voice froze Holly to the spot; somewhere between a scream and a moan. Holly looked up to the platform at the far side of the room, where Greg should have been working.

But the sofa was kicked back on to two legs. The cushions were thrown all around. Greg stood still as a statue. His arms were straight by his side. Tom Stone stood behind him. His face was close against Greg's, almost resting on his shoulder. In his right hand, Stone held a gun. It sat there steady and gleaming, centimetres from Greg's forehead!

12   *The master disk*

'Come on in!' Tom greeted them as if he was inviting them to a party. His glance didn't even flicker sideways. He kept his gaze firmly fixed on Greg. 'Come in!' he insisted. 'But don't bother to shut the door!'

'Do as he says!' Greg told them. His face was ashen with fear. He didn't move his head, but his eyes swung wildly in their direction.

Holly edged forward stiff as wood. She almost stumbled and fell. Tom's gun moved a fraction closer to Greg's head.

'Keep the noise down!' he muttered.

The girls sidled around the debris. 'Where's Sharon?' Holly whispered, not daring to take her eyes off Tom.

'Here I am!' The door clicked shut behind them. The voice was unmistakable.

Holly and Steffie froze. They stared straight ahead, waiting for Sharon Hall to emerge from her hiding-place behind the door. When she did, the gun in her hand was the only thing Holly saw.

She smiled from behind the gun. 'So!' She aimed it slowly at Holly, then slid it round to catch Steffie in her sights.

Sharon Hall was dressed for action in tight black trousers and top. Her flame-coloured hair was tied back, but it caught the lamplight in a blaze of coppery red. 'No need to move,' she said calmly. 'Just hold it there!'

Holly glanced at Greg. She swallowed hard, though her mouth felt rough and dry. They were trapped and there was absolutely nothing they could do!

'You look surprised!' Sharon Hall mocked. Her mouth was a wide, smiling gash of red. Her fingernails shone red as they wrapped themselves even more firmly around her silver gun. She held it in a double-handed grip at arm's length. 'All that work you did to keep Greg out of our hands! It's all come to nothing. What a pity!'

Holly felt the wave of disappointment wash over her. It was like running a race until your lungs were almost bursting, then finding out that you'd come last.

'I expect you want to know how we found you!' Sharon gloated.

She was enjoying herself, Holly realised. She was enjoying their pale, shocked faces and horror-stricken eyes. She wanted to make this moment last!

'Simple!' Sharon kept them within her sights, but she backed off slowly towards the platform where Stone still held Greg prisoner. 'OK, so we lost you earlier today.' She wrinkled her nose. 'But you didn't think we'd just give in and call it a day? She came up to Greg, almost flirting with him. 'We were so close,' she mocked. 'I couldn't just give you up!'

Greg looked helplessly at her. Tom's gun held steady.

'Well,' Sharon went on. 'We sat in the car and did a little thinking. We decided to back off up that farm track by the cliff. Back to base, to find out where you lived, Holly. You were so busy giving directions to Greg in that old minibus, I felt sure you must know exactly where you were headed!' She paused and smiled. 'I figured that all we had to do was to go back to school and hang around some more, until we could collar some kids.' She paused to let this sink in. 'There were plenty hanging around. All we had to do was to ask where Holly Adams lived!'

Holly breathed in sharply.

'I said I was your long-lost aunt, come to pay you a visit.' Sharon put her head to one side. 'Cute, isn't it? The way I told it, it was perfectly possible!'

Holly stared back at her through narrowed eyes. She was too clever, too determined for them after all. They stood there, still as a photograph, unable to move.

'Let them go, Sharon!' Greg broke the silence. 'They haven't done anything! Why do you need them? Talk to me, but let them go!'

Tom Stone sniggered. 'Now that would be messy,' he said. 'And I like things to be neat!'

'He does.' Sharon Hall laughed. 'He's the neatest killer I ever met!'

Holly shuddered. She felt more and more hopeless. It was the casual way Sharon said things that got to her. How could she do this and seem to enjoy it?

'Send those two over here to me!' Stone said sharply.

Sharon waved her gun at them. 'You heard the man!' she said.

Holly and Steffie stumbled through the heaps of wood towards the platform.

'Come up!' Sharon Hall ordered. 'Let's have you all nicely together in a bunch, where we can keep an eye on you!'

Again they followed instructions, though Holly seemed to have to send conscious messages to her brain to make her legs work, even to breathe. Eventually, she stood shoulder to shoulder with Steffie and Greg.

Sharon Hall looked at them all, one eye closed, using the gun barrel to reset her aim. 'What gets me,' she said to Greg, 'is how you ever thought you could keep that disk!' She fixed her gun on him. 'If only you'd seen it my way when we were going out together. You could have let me in on MOON MAZE then and saved us all a lot of trouble!' Her voice was sing-song, sneering.

Greg stared back without flinching. A nerve twitched in his neck. He held his head up. 'You never cared for me at all, did you? Right from the start you were just spying for Megaware!'

Sharon Hall sighed. 'I see the trouble with you, I guess. You're new to all this, Greg! Megaware is my life, you see. When Megaware's in trouble, I'm in trouble too. I'd do anything to stop them going under! And when I saw you collecting all that loot for SPACE WALK, your very first game, it made me mad!' Yes, you're right, I was never the least bit interested in Greg Smith as a person! I'd do anything to get MOON MAZE from you!'

Greg nodded slowly.

'Absolutely anything!' She aimed again; menacing, cold hearted.

Greg glanced at Holly and Steffie. Then he spoke out and admitted defeat. 'OK, you win! You're the best! No one can beat you!' He nodded as he spoke. Tom Stone's gun wavered, but his grip on Greg didn't loosen.

'You give in?' Sharon Hall was taken aback. The possibility hadn't entered her head. 'You'll hand over the master disk?' Still she kept the gun trained on the group.

'Have it!' Greg muttered. 'I've been working round the clock in that lousy hideout and now it's finished!' He pulled the blue disk out of his pocket and held it out to her. 'Keep it! You hear, I give in!'

Holly heard Steffie begin to sob quietly.

'You mean it?' Sharon Hall edged forward, her face smiling in disbelief. 'Say it again!' She put out her hand to take the disk. Holly noticed that it trembled and her eyes were fixed on the disk as if hypnotised.

Steffie sobbed.

'Watch it!' Tom Stone warned. He put the metal of his gun right up against Greg's temple. 'He might not mean it! Maybe it's not the right disk! Don't trust him!'

Sharon Hall paused. Her smile faded.

'I mean it!' Greg said steadily. Tom Stone had forced his head backwards, but he couldn't break his nerve. 'Do what you like. Make your millions. OK?'

Falteringly, Sharon held on to the disk. She looked dazed. 'Tom's right,' she said slowly. 'You've tricked us before. Give me that machine. I need to see if this really is MOON MAZE!'

She made Greg go over to fetch his computer, shadowed every inch of the way by Tom Stone.

He brought it back, set a table upright on its legs, and put the machine on it. Slowly Sharon came forward. For a second she seemed to forget all about Steffie and Holly.

Holly looked round the room. The whole place was in chaos. Upturned furniture lay all around. One table lamp had been sent crashing down. Another toppled precariously against a wall, its wire snaking across the floor. It was the only light left. Holly stiffened as an idea clicked. Could she make a move?

But Sharon caught her intention. 'Come over here!' she snapped at the girls, waving her gun. 'We don't want you getting into any trouble over there. Come and have a sneak preview of Megaware's latest computer game!' She turned to Greg. 'And it had better be what you say it is, believe me!'

Calm again, she slotted the disk into the computer and grabbed hold of Holly's arm. 'I expect you're good at this. Come and demonstrate it for us!' She shoved Holly on to a chair in front of the machine.

Holly felt numb. With shaking fingers she pressed the keys to operate the game. A bright blue light flooded the screen, then a spaceman appeared in his silver suit. He sat trapped in the middle of a maze. 'Starware Ltd.' flashed across the bottom of the screen, and the multicoloured

169

words, 'MOON MAZE', exploded over the space-man's head.

'Yes!' Sharon let out a hiss of triumph. 'At last! The master disk!' She pressed the eject button, grabbed the disk and turned off the machine.

'Let's make double sure!' Tom said. 'Let me finish him for you right here! Get this thing over with! No more Greg Smith! No more Starware!' There was a sickening click inside the mechanism of the gun.

'No!' Steffie screamed. 'He's given you the disk! That's what you want, isn't it?' She hid her face in her hands and collapsed forward on to the floor.

Holly saw Sharon's face go blank. 'But he's smart. He'd beat me in the end,' Sharon said. She turned away. 'OK, go ahead,' she said to Tom Stone in a flat, deadly voice.

In that split second Holly acted.

She hooked her leg around the loose wire that snaked across the floor. She wrenched hard. The table light crashed to the floor and plunged the room in darkness.

'Run!' she yelled. People screamed and yelled and swore. A gun went off. 'Run!' Holly screamed again. 'Get help, someone!'

She felt herself dragged to the floor. She kicked and bit.

A torchlight pierced the darkness. It showed Holly that she was in the clutches of Tom Stone. It lit up Greg crawling over the floor to grab Steffie and bundle her to safety across the room. Holly heard Tracy's voice yelling from the doorway; 'Holly, where are you? I can't see you!' She flashed the beam around the room.

'Over here!' she screamed. Her arms and legs flailed against the stocky, muscular body of her attacker. He was much stronger. She was losing the fight. 'Help, Tracy!'

'This way!' Belinda's voice yelled now above all the noise. 'This way, Steffie, Greg!' Her torch-beam revealed a clear passage for them through the debris of fallen wood and upset furniture. She kept it firmly focused on them.

'Holly!' Tracy was still trying desperately to reach her, but a gun went off; once, twice. Bullets ricocheted off a metal surface and rang out. Tracy fell silent. Even Holly froze.

Then, cursing, Tom Stone picked himself up from the floor. He dragged Holly with him. 'Get out of my way!' he roared. He seized Holly round the neck and shoulder, dragged her with him and charged blindly for the door. Weak and helpless, Holly couldn't resist. Within seconds he'd pulled her out into the yard. Holly felt the fresh air, saw stars above. Everything whirled and spun crazily.

'Holly!' Tracy screamed again. 'Belinda, he's got Holly!'

Footsteps, shouts. Then, from another direction, sirens!

'It's the police!' Belinda yelled. 'Everyone stop where you are!'

In the moonlight, dark figures ran here and there across the yard. Holly felt Tom Stone haul her along the side of the workshop and over a low wall. He kept one hand over her mouth, the gun against her ribs.

The sounds from the house grew fainter. Holly could feel firm ground underfoot. Her legs ran unwillingly over tarmac to keep pace with Tom Stone. 'Make a sound and you're dead!' he grunted. His chest heaved, his foot caught in the gutter, but he ran clumsily on. Twice they fell and twice he jerked Holly to her feet. He dragged her further and further down the lane, away from the cottage.

She managed to twist round and caught a glimpse of the house lights going on. All voices had died away now, out of earshot. Still she and Stone staggered down the lane. In the moonlight, his silver car lay waiting. No one to help. No one to cry out to.

She was alone with a killer.

No; she was not quite alone. Footsteps stumbled along behind them. Sharon Hall had followed and caught them up.

Without a word, breathless and desperate, she joined them.

Tom Stone opened the car door and shoved

Holly inside. 'You got the disk?' he said roughly to Sharon.

She held it up. 'Of course! Here, keep it safe!' She gave it to her accomplice, who buttoned it inside his shirt pocket.

Holly, slumped across the back seat of the car, began to wrench at the door handle opposite. It was locked.

'Oh, no you don't!' Sharon jumped in beside her and held her back, while Stone leaped into the front seat and started up the engine. 'Whatever happens next, we need you, Holly Adams!' Her gun was trained, her mouth stretched into a cruel smile. 'You're our safe passage out of here.'

Holly felt herself flung forward in the seat as Stone slammed the car into reverse. 'Let's get out of here!' he muttered. They swung round in the lane and set off again with a screech of tyres.

'No!' Holly cried out. They had her and they had MOON MAZE. They were going to get away!

13 High Almscliff

A huge bank of clouds drifted over the face of the moon. The landscape darkened as the silver car lurched down the lane on to the main road.

'Listen!' Sharon had the window open and she looked back down the lane. Another car engine roared, the blue beam of a police light pierced the darkness. 'They're coming after us!'

Stone pressed the accelerator. The car sped on towards a deserted Willow Dale.

'Faster!' Sharon yelled. 'Go up past the school, take a turn here! We've got to lose them!'

Without a seat belt, Holly was flung from side to side. She clung to the front seat as the car swerved right. They raced past the library, past the petrol station and began to head out of town once more. Holly glimpsed the school; a huge, shadowy place, well out of range of the orange streetlights. The scream of police sirens still trailed them.

'Where to?' Stone shouted. He wrenched at the steering-wheel, squealed round a bend, and headed up on to the moor road. 'Where are we heading?'

Sharon stared out of the back window. She gripped the seat to brace herself as the car swung almost out of control. 'I think we fooled them!' she said. The sirens faded, lost somewhere down in the town centre. 'Head straight on. We'll cut across country. This road leads to a bypass. Just keep going!' She turned and settled into her seat.

Holly closed her eyes. She felt the powerful car surge up the hill. When she opened them, the streetlights had ended and the black space of moorland stretched to either side. She looked out and felt completely alone.

Then headlights dipped and curved towards them, a long way off, two white dots steadily approaching.

Stone flinched and gripped the wheel.

'It's nothing, just an ordinary car. Keep going!' Sharon ordered.

The lights bobbed and glared, closer and closer.

Their own car dropped into a hollow then began to climb. The other car's lights were almost on top of them now, suddenly blinding them.

'Dip those lights!' Stone bellowed. But they dazzled him. A blue light came on and wailed out its warning.

'Police!' Sharon screamed as the headlights bore down and the blue light flashed.

Tom Stone pulled wide of the oncoming car. He hit a grass verge, braked and skidded. Holly clung on for dear life. More brakes squealed. She was thrown forward. Stone swerved again, clear of the other car. Then there was a rasping sound of metal crunching against rock, a helpless whirring of wheels and finally silence.

For a moment, all was still. Tom Stone rested his head against the steering-wheel. Sharon had her eyes closed. Then she opened them. Shaken but unhurt, she quickly took stock. 'Right, let's go!' With a firm grip on Holly's wrist, she flung open the door. She dragged her, bruised and shocked, out into the dark night. Fifty metres down the road the police car lay nose down in a ditch. There was no sign of life.

'What now?' Tom clambered out of the passenger door and kicked it shut.

'We go on foot,' Sharon said. 'Come on, let's go!'

'What do you mean? They've got cars, they're everywhere!' he protested.

'So we go cross country!' Sharon insisted. 'All three of us. We'll lose them in the dark and we'll be long gone by the time they get themselves together!' Grimly she thrust Holly into Stone's strong hold and they set off across the moor.

'Keep up!' she urged Holly. She wrenched her back on her feet after she and Tom stumbled against a boulder. 'Don't think you can escape. Come on!'

'This way! This way!' Tom shouted. They staggered on.

Holly ran between them, her forehead cold and damp, the nape of her neck wet with sweat. She'd never known darkness so deep or fear so numbing. When she fell again, they dragged her back on to her feet. When she cried with pain and exhaustion, they shoved and swore. 'Stop!' she gasped. 'Please stop!'

'No, keep moving!' Tom commanded. He seemed more confident now, unafraid of the dark.

The shadows were dense black. There was no horizon, no difference between sky and land.

'I can hear them!' Sharon gasped. 'Listen, I can hear them following us again!'

They paused. The wind blew against Holly's wet face, stronger here on top of the moor. And yes, there were sounds; sharp orders being called, faint beams of light way down by the road.

'We can still beat them!' Tom promised. 'Keep going!'

They ran again, across bare earth, sandy and scattered with rocks. Where were they? Holly's pounding heart skipped. Where were they?

They ran into sheer rock! Tom Stone put his hand out against the cold, dark surface. He looked up at blackness. 'This way!' He dragged Holly sideways.

She looked up. She felt the massive, cold rock rising high above them. It smelled dank. Tom stopped and reached out again; the same tall, dark wall of rock lay in front of them. He looked at Sharon. 'What is this place?' he demanded, delivering Holly into her grasp and running frantically along the base of the cliff.

'Where are we?' Sharon hissed. 'Come on, come on! Where are we?'

Holly felt the sheer, cold rock. 'High Almscliff!' she said. She knew this was the only place it could be; a horseshoe of rock fifteen metres high, with a narrow entrance and no way through. It was a massive, terrible place, bare and dreary by daylight; at night impossible to get out of without a light. 'It's a dead end!' she told Sharon Hall with a gleam of triumph, a sudden surge of hope.

'Tom!' Sharon almost screamed. 'We've got to cut back out of here. The kid says this goes nowhere!'

'I know that!' He came running back. 'Do you think I don't know that!'

He looked up. A white crescent of moon had reappeared out of the bank of black clouds. Then he looked back the way they'd come. The beams of light were closing in, the policemen were shouting loud enough to startle hidden animals; maybe sheep, out on the moor. They lumbered off through the heather. The police had reached the brow of the hill. Holly could barely see their silhouettes in the faint moonlight. Then there was darkness again, as more cloud raced across the moon.

'Let's go back!' Sharon yelled. 'We've got to cut back!'

It's too late!' Tom said. 'We go up!' He gestured roughly towards the cliff-face. 'Up and over the top. They'll never follow us!'

'Up!' Sharon Hall gasped. 'We can't!'

Holly felt her head reel at the thought; up High Almscliff at night! Did he want to kill them all?

'You want them to get us?' Stone demanded. 'You're crazy!' he said.

Sharon's resistance caved in. 'OK, let's go!' She gripped a ledge of rock and began to climb. Her breath already came in short, panicky gasps.

And the nightmare went on. Tom Stone dug his gun in Holly's ribs and ordered her up the rock-face. There were ledges and crevices for footholds, if you could find them in the dark. Slowly Holly edged upwards and soon drew level with Sharon.

She went on ahead, groping the rough surface of the black rock, thankful for clumps of grass or heather to heave herself up with. She kept her cheek pressed against the cliff-face, fearful of tipping backwards into dark space. Her hands began to bleed, her trousers scraped and tore on jagged points. But still she climbed; in sheer terror she drove herself on.

Once she dared to look down. There was Sharon

Hall pinned to a ledge many feet below. Her gun stuck out from the waistband of her trousers, leaving both hands free to climb, but she was struggling to make progress. Tom was a far better climber. He shoved the gun against Holly's side again and reached for the next handhold.

Holly's gaze swept the ground. There were lights at the base of the cliff now. They swooped and flashed against the sheer face like a weird semaphore. Police officers shouted and pointed. She thought she heard Tracy's voice give a startled cry. But Tom dragged her so hard she half lost her balance. One foot slipped. She gave a harsh gasp deep in her throat, then recovered her footing. She was forced to climb on.

Loose stones dislodged and peppered the rockface. She spat gravel out of her mouth. She didn't know how much further she could climb like this. She didn't dare think of reaching the top and of what would happen once they got there!

'Tom!' Sharon shouted. She seemed a long way down. Her voice sounded strange. 'Wait!'

'Keep moving!' he yelled.

'I can't! I can't move!' She was desperate.

Tom thrust back his head and gritted his teeth. 'What d'you mean, you can't move? Just put your foot on the next ledge; keep moving!'

But Sharon cried. It was the small cry of a child, mixed with a sob. 'I'm scared, Tom! I can't move!'

Holly could hear Sharon's breath coming in loud, short gasps, in panicky bursts. She tried to peer back down, but Tom jabbed her ribs. He swore.

'Oh God, I'm scared!' Sharon wailed. She'd completely lost control. 'You can't make me do this, Tom! I'm not going to make it!'

'Sure you will!' he yelled savagely. He twisted wide of his ledge to look down at her. More loose stones rattled to the ground. Sharon screamed.

'Oh God, help!'

Holly stared at Tom Stone. What now?

A policeman's searchlight hit them full in the face as they clung for dear life to their ledge. Tom looked pale as death. 'Keep climbing!' he snarled at Holly. 'I've got the disk here in my pocket. That's all that matters. We're not going down to get her, OK!'

Holly groaned. He'd ditched Sharon without a second thought. When it came to it, he'd left Sharon to her fate. Holly's muscles ached. Her head was spinning in the glare of the searchlight.

'Tom!' Sharon wailed again.

'Move!' Tom yelled at Holly in a mad rage. 'You hear me!' He made a sudden sideways lunge.

But he misjudged it. He pushed too far. Holly pressed herself against the rock and felt his heavy arm brush down her back. He struggled to regain his balance. The gun slipped from his hand as he scrabbled for a hold; a root, a ledge, anything! But

181

this time there was nothing. Tom Stone's weight fell sideways. His arms flailed. His whole body toppled and fell.

There was no scream, no sound at all, until Tom hit the ground.

Sharon Hall curled up on her ledge and whimpered.

Holly closed her eyes. When she opened them, she expected Tom Stone's brutal face to be there still, snarling at her, telling her to go on!

But it was a policeman, strapped to the rock with ropes and cradles. He'd been lowered to Holly's position from the top of High Almscliff. He took her in his arms. 'You're safe,' he said. 'Just hold on to me!'

Tom Stone was taken to hospital under police guard. They said he was unconscious, with head and leg injuries. He would probably recover.

Sharon Hall gave Holly one cold, expressionless look before she was driven off. She had only one weakness, Holly realised; a fear of heights. And Tom Stone must have known it. It made his betrayal all the greater. But now she was hard again, back in control.

Tracy and Belinda came silently up to Holly as she stood and watched Sharon Hall being hustled away by the police. They each took one hand and waited until Holly was ready to talk.

'How are you?' Belinda asked gently.

Holly felt the firm grip of her friends on either side. 'I'm OK,' she said with a faint smile. 'How about Greg and Steffie?'

'They're fine!' Belinda told her. 'They're waiting for us back at the cottage.'

Holly began to walk slowly away from High Almscliff; surrounded by friends, ambulance workers, policemen.

'When did you realise something had gone wrong?' she asked Tracy.

'If you wake up, and you hear furniture crashing around in the workshop; you know something's wrong!' Tracy exclaimed.

'We phoned the police straightaway and raced across. Then we saw the light go out and heard shots!' Belinda said. 'We only had torches with us. I didn't think we had much of a chance against a gun!'

'Two guns!' Holly said. She was tired out. 'Anyway, good timing!' She smiled at them both.

'Not quite good enough,' Tracy said. 'Tom had already grabbed you!'

But Holly didn't want to relive the last half-hour just yet. 'So,' she said, and sighed. 'As long as everyone's OK!'

They tucked her, Tracy and Belinda into a police car and drove them back to Holly's house. Greg and Steffie greeted them at the door. Questions and paperwork would wait until morning, they said.

Holly found herself sitting at home in her kitchen with her friends. No one said much. Relief flooded the room, and 'thank you' didn't seem to cover everything Greg and Steffie wanted to say.

The newspapers all carried giant headlines: 'MILLION DOLLAR MAN!'

'Software superstar, Greg Smith, loves success after all!' the article began. 'He plans to come out of retirement to sell his new game. MOON MAZE will make him millions of dollars worldwide.'

'Main rival, Megaware International, now admit that it's no contest. They have no new game of their own to sell, despite recent rumours to the contrary.

'Twenty-two year old Greg sets off tomorrow on a whirlwind tour of Europe and the States to promote his new product.'

Somewhere, on an inside page, a smaller headline reported the arrest of two computer experts, a man and a woman, on abduction and firearms offences. The crimes had taken place in the picture-postcard Yorkshire town of Willow Dale. Sharon Hall and Tom Stone were former employees of Megaware International. The giant software firm denied any involvement with the pair's criminal activities.

'Former employees!' Holly stared over the top of her newspaper at Greg. 'Wow!'

He nodded. 'They dropped them double quick!' he confirmed.

'And you don't think they'll send anyone else after you?' Steffie checked.

'Not now. The game's over for them.' Greg grinned broadly. 'Thanks to you lot from the Mystery Club.'

'What's this about a whirlwind tour of the States?' his sister demanded.

He blushed. 'I thought I might just hop across the Atlantic for a few days, get things moving over there,' he said.

'Hop across the Atlantic!' Steffie echoed. 'Million Dollar Man!'

'Any more of that and I'll stop the cheque for the new school minibus!' Greg threatened.

'The new school minibus!' Holly exclaimed. The others sat open-mouthed.'

He shrugged. 'It's a donation. It's the least I could do after I took the old one!' He picked up the coffee-pot. 'More coffee anyone?' he said.

They let the news sink in. 'Oh, and while we're at it,' Steffie said. She smiled broadly. 'Since we're all being generous and grateful and everything; I've been thinking about something else, Holly!'

'Yes?' She eyed Steffie cautiously.

'I thought it was time I offered you a proper job at *Winformation*,' Steffie said.

Holly leaped to her feet. 'A proper job!' she repeated.

Tracy and Belinda tried to hold on to her, but she began to jig around the table with excitement.

'What! What!' she demanded.

'How about being sub-editor?' Steffie said. 'For a trial period?'

'Sub-editor!' Holly squealed and fell backwards on to the sofa, clutching her crumpled newspaper. Her mind raced with ideas for the magazine. 'OK, but listen, Steffie; I think we should change the magazine's title to something more modern!' She jumped back on to her feet. 'I'm sure there are loads of changes we could make!'

But Steffie looked back at her severely. She glanced at the others, then launched off; 'Now look, Holly Adams, just because you've been here five minutes, don't think you can waltz in and wreck years of tradition!'

Greg, Tracy and Belinda laughed. Steffie joined in. But Holly's eyes widened. She couldn't wait for the half-term holiday to finish. She wanted to be back at school, looking for another good mystery to report; another great scoop!

CROSSED LINES

by Fiona Kelly

Holly, Belinda and Tracy are back in the
tenth thrilling adventure in the
Mystery Club series, published by
Hodder Children's Books.

Here is the first chapter . . .

1 The voice on the telephone

Oh, no! *Now* what? Holly looked up from her book at the sound of the doorbell. She was beginning to suspect there was a conspiracy to try and disturb her as much as possible.

It had taken her most of the morning to read just a couple of chapters of her new P. J. Benson mystery book, what with all the workmen clumping about hammering and drilling and shouting instructions to one another.

With a sigh, Holly clambered off her bed, tucking her hair behind her ears as she slapped the book down on the duvet and headed downstairs.

Holly had quickly discovered that house-sitting and reading didn't mix.

It didn't help, either, that the electricity had been temporarily turned off and that all the outside doors were wide open to allow the workmen in and out.

A chilling winter breeze was cutting its way along the hall as Holly came down the stairs.

This is a really brilliant time of year to turn the house

into an open-plan igloo! she thought. *Just when it's about to snow!*

Holly was fond of snow. She was looking forward to seeing the rolling Yorkshire hills transformed by a blanket of pure white. But as she came shivering down the stairs, she couldn't help wishing that it was summer.

The front door was wide open. A man in a heavy brown coat was standing on the doorstep. He looked to be in his thirties, with red-framed spectacles and a chubby face, his pale hair combed in an attempt to conceal his balding head. He held a clipboard across one forearm and as Holly approached he was busy gnawing at the end of a ballpoint pen.

'Mr Adams?' asked the man.

Holly smiled. 'No. *Miss* Adams,' she said. 'My dad's out. Did you want to speak to him?'

The man extended a plump hand. 'Tony Blake,' he said. Holly shook his soft, warm hand. 'From Gardener, Preston and Blake. The surveyors. Your father was expecting me.'

'Oh, yes.' Holly remembered. Along with countless other instructions, Mr Adams had told her to expect a man from the company of surveyors who were overseeing the work on the house. 'My dad won't be back for a while,' she told Tony Blake. 'He said you could have a look round, if you like, and he'll talk to you as soon as he arrives home. Is that OK?'

Tony Blake nodded. 'Yes, that's fine.'

'Do you want me to show you around?' asked Holly.

'No, no. That's all right,' said Tony Blake. 'I'll find my own way around.' He smiled. 'Don't worry about me. You carry on doing whatever you were doing.'

A chance would be a fine thing, thought Holly, as a burst of hammering came echoing up from the cellar. She heard the deep bark of a dog from somewhere outside.

Tony Blake looked over his shoulder towards a small white van parked at the kerb. Holly saw a long muzzle poking out through the misted-up and slightly opened window.

'I always bring Luther with me,' explained Tony Blake. He shouted down the path. 'Luther! Be quiet. Behave!'

'Will he be OK in there?' asked Holly.

'Yes,' said Tony Blake. 'He'll be fine once he settles down.' He smiled. 'He's better than any car alarm. No one's ever going to steal my van, that's for sure.'

'No,' said Holly. 'I suppose not. Give me a shout if you need anything.'

'Will do,' said Tony Blake.

Holly went back upstairs and picked up her book.

The door opened and a workman's face appeared.

'Oops, sorry,' he said. 'Wrong room.' He closed the door again and she heard him stamp off across the landing.

Holly gave an exasperated laugh. 'It *is*,' she said to herself. 'It's a *conspiracy* to stop me reading this book.'

Both Holly and Miranda had always loved mystery novels and P. J. Benson was far and away their favourite writer. The shelves in Holly's bedroom were crammed with books, but right then she would have happily sold the lot for just half an hour's peace and quiet with her new one.

She curled up on the bed.

'Chapter Three. The thing in the attic,' she read. 'Juliana Moon crept to the head of the stairs. The attic door stood closed in front of her. The room beyond had been unused, so she had been told, for twenty years. But she had heard noises from up there. She stepped forward and reached for the handle, trembling at the thought of what might lurk within.'

Holly's bedroom door came bursting open, nearly startling her out of her skin.

'Surprise!' yelled Belinda. 'We've come to keep you company!'

Tracy followed her in. 'We're here to rescue you from boredom,' she said. 'The front door was open so we just came right up. It's freezing out, isn't it? I'm never going to get used to this climate of yours.'

Holly laughed, flinging her book over her shoulder on to the bed. 'I give up,' she said.

Belinda pulled her coat off and plumped down on the bed.

'Aren't you pleased to see us?' she asked. 'We thought you'd be bored to death, having to stay in all day with nothing to do.'

'Of course she's pleased to see us,' said Tracy. 'So? 'What are we going to do?'

'We could think up some more ideas for that mystery board game of ours,' said Belinda. It was an idea they had been working on for some time.

Holly dragged the prototype board out from under her bed and the three girls sat in a circle on the floor.

They had not been at it for long when the phone rang.

It was Mrs Adams calling from work to remind Holly to give Jamie a ring to tell him to get home to do his chores. Somehow housework didn't have the same hold over Jamie as spending the day playing on his friend Philip Owen's computer.

Holly told her mother she'd give him a ring. She was standing in the kitchen trying to find Philip's phone number on the memo board when Belinda and Tracy came down.

'We're a bit peckish,' said Belinda. 'Any chance of a slice of toast or two?'

'*You're* a bit peckish, you mean,' said Tracy. 'I'd just like some herbal tea.'

'No chance of that,' said Holly. 'The electricity has been turned off. We can't boil the kettle. You'll have to make do with some orange juice or something.'

Tracy sidled up to Holly. 'Who's the guy with the clipboard?' she whispered. Holly looked over her shoulder. Tony Blake was in the hall just outside the kitchen door, apparently busily engaged in writing notes.

Holly explained who he was.

'A surveyor?' said Belinda. 'That's a good sign, isn't it? If you've got surveyors in, doesn't it mean the work's almost done?'

'I *wish*,' sighed Holly.

She found Philip's phone number and dialled.

'There's bread in the bin,' she told Belinda. 'And some cheese in the fridge.'

'Great,' said Belinda. 'Cheese sandwiches. Got any pickle?'

Holly put the receiver to her ear. 'There's some funny noises going on down here,' she said, frowning at a series of whirrs and clicks on the line.

'Perhaps someone's drilled through the phone line?' said Tracy. 'I wouldn't be surprised. We had a guy in to fix the lights in our sitting-room once.

After he'd gone we tried the switch and every light in the house went off. It was a week before we got things back to normal.'

'No,' said Holly. 'It's OK. I can hear it ringing.'

Mrs Owen picked up the phone. Holly asked to speak to Jamie. In the silence that followed Mrs Owen putting down the receiver, Holly heard a regular burring sound, as if she had a crossed line and someone else was trying to dial.

'There's definitely something wrong here,' said Holly. 'Come and listen.'

The three girls crowded round the receiver.

As they listened, the burring stopped with a loud click and they heard a tinny voice.

'That's an answering machine,' said Belinda. 'You must have a fault on your line.'

'I'd better put the phone down and dial again,' said Holly.

'That won't work,' said Belinda. 'If the phone is off the hook at the other end you'll still be connected, whatever you do.'

'Shhh!' said Tracy. 'Listen!'

The answering machine message had ended and the clear voice of an excited-sounding woman could be heard.

'It's Tessa,' said the voice. 'I'm in Brompton. I think I've found out where there's a copy of the book with the Duke's poem in it. In the very village where it all took place. It looks like we're finally going to discover where the amulet was hidden. I'll phone you back at three o'clock to confirm. I shan't be able to get over there for a few days. Speak to you later, I hope. Bye.'

There was a brief hum and then the line seemed to clear.

'I wonder what that was all about?' said Tracy. 'She sounded very pleased with herself, whatever it was.'

'It's none of our business,' said Belinda. 'It's not very polite to eavesdrop on other people's conversations.'

'We were hardly eavesdropping,' said Holly.

'What do you want?' came Jamie's voice down the phone. He sounded less than pleased at being disturbed.

'Mum says you're to come home and do your chores,' said Holly.

'I'm busy,' said Jamie. 'Tell her you couldn't find me. I'll do them all tomorrow.'

'I'm not telling her anything of the sort,' said Holly. 'You get over here, pest, or there'll be trouble.'

A loud groan sounded down the phone.

'Tell you what,' said Holly. 'Come over straight away and I'll do you some lunch, how's that?'

Jamie grumbled something that Holly didn't quite catch and put the phone down.

Belinda gave Holly a beaming smile. 'Did some-one mention lunch?' she said. 'That's the best idea I've heard since breakfast.'

Holly grinned. 'OK,' she said. 'We might as well all have lunch – at least the gas is connected. But if Jamie's not back in half an hour I'm going to phone Mum and tell her.'

The three girls were just laying the table for lunch when Jamie came in, sniffing the air like a hound.

'What have you cooked me?' he asked.

'Sausage, egg, baked beans, mushrooms and tomatoes,' recited Belinda, filling four plates. She grinned. 'Just what we need to keep the cold out.'

Jamie slumped on to a chair. 'I'm exhausted,' he said. He grinned. 'Philip's got a mega-brilliant new computer game. I'm going to do my chores as quick as I can, then I'm going back over there. His mum said I can stay over for the night.'

'If your room's not tidy by the time Dad gets back you won't be going anywhere,' said Holly.

The four of them sat down to eat.

'You'd better tell Philip's mother there's some-thing wrong with her phone when you go back,' said Tracy.

Jamie looked at her, his mouth full of sausage. 'Like what?' he mumbled.

'We heard a crossed line,' said Holly.

'What did you hear?' asked Jamie. 'Anything interesting?'

'Not especially,' began Holly, but Tracy interrupted her.

'A woman left a message on an answering machine,' she said. 'Something about a book and a duke and an amulet.'

Jamie frowned. 'What's an amulet?'

'It's a sort of pendant that hangs from a necklace,' said Belinda. 'A kind of good-luck charm.'

'What did she say about it?' asked Jamie.

'Not much,' said Tracy. 'She said she'd phone the person back at three o'clock to explain.'

A grin expanded across Jamie's face. 'Are you going to listen in?'

'Certainly not,' said Holly. She frowned at Tracy. 'I wasn't going to mention any of this in front of *him*,' she said. 'You know how nosy he is.'

'I am not,' said Jamie. 'You three are the nosy ones round here. You just don't want me to know, 'cos you think there's some big mystery about it and you don't want to let me in on it. I bet you're going to listen in at three o'clock.'

'For the last time,' said Holly, 'we're *not* going to listen in.' She heard footsteps and turned to see Tony Blake come into the kitchen.

He smiled. 'Sorry to disturb you,' he said. 'Something smells good. I've just got to check a few things in here, if that's all right.'

'Of course,' said Holly. 'How's it going? Is everything looking OK?'

Tony Blake nodded. 'With any luck all the major work should be finished in a few weeks,' he said.

While they finished eating, Tony Blake wandered around the kitchen scribbling notes down on his clipboard.

The girls stacked the plates and Holly turned to Jamie.

'You can wash up,' she told him. 'And then you'd better get down to some work before Dad gets home.'

'Yes, sir,' said Jamie, giving her a mock salute. 'Any more orders, sir?'

Holly shook her head. 'You're such a comedian, Jamie.' She looked round at her friends. 'Coming?' she asked.

The three girls went back up to Holly's room to carry on planning their board game.

Some time later they heard the sound of the vacuum cleaner from Jamie's room.

'That's good,' said Holly. 'At least the electricity is back on. That means we can boil the kettle for a hot drink.'

She crossed the landing to Jamie's room.

'Jamie? Do you want a drink of . . .' Her voice trailed off. The vacuum cleaner was lying on the carpet in the middle of his room, roaring away.

But there was no sign of Jamie. Puzzled, she switched it off.

Where was he? And why should he have left the cleaner on? A sudden suspicion dawned in Holly's mind. She glanced at the clock on Jamie's bedside table.

Three minutes past three. Three minutes after the time that the woman had said she would be phoning again on that crossed line.

Holly ran downstairs.

She nearly bumped into Tony Blake, who was standing just outside the kitchen door.

'Sorry,' she said. 'Excuse me.'

Jamie was sitting at the table, the telephone receiver to his ear, his hand over the mouthpiece as he scribbled something on a sheet of paper.

'Jamie!' shouted Holly.

He made frantic signs to her to keep quiet. Ignoring him, she slammed her hand down on the button that cut the telephone line.

'Jamie!' yelled Holly. 'What do you think you're doing?'

'Hey!' Jamie glared at her. 'What did you do that for?'

'To stop you eavesdropping,' said Holly. 'I told you not to.'

'No, you didn't,' said Jamie. 'You just said *you* weren't going to. I've missed the end of what she was saying now, thanks to you!'

'Good!' said Holly. 'You shouldn't have been listening in the first place.'

'You won't say that when you find out what I've heard,' said Jamie. 'Look.' He waved the sheet of paper in front of her.

She looked at what he had written.

The Bad Luck Duke. Very valuable amulet. Gilchrist's Bookshop. Poetry book. Two days' time. Catching 3.15 train from Brompton. Should arrive 3.45.

Holly grabbed the sheet of paper from him and screwed it up in her fist.

'Don't do that!' yelled Jamie. 'Didn't you see? She said the Bad Luck Duke's amulet was incredibly valuable. We could look for it. We've got enough clues now.' He looked excitedly at her. 'There might be a reward for finding it,' he said. 'We could split the money.

'No, we can't,' said Holly. 'You can't listen in on other people's conversations like that, Jamie. It's wrong.' She walked over to the rubbish bin, lifted the lid, and dropped the screwed up sheet of paper inside.

'I hate you, Holly Adams,' said Jamie. 'I know what you're up to. You want this mystery all to yourself!'

'No, I don't,' said Holly. 'It's nothing to do with us. Forget about it, Jamie. Now, you'd better get up there and finish your room, or I'll tell Dad what you've been up to, and you *will* be in trouble.'

With a final defiant glare, Jamie stamped upstairs.

As she left the kitchen, Holly saw that Tony Blake was still standing outside the door. He must have heard everything. He gave her a sympathetic smile.

'Kid brothers, eh?' he said.

'Tell me about it,' sighed Holly. 'Still, my dad should be home soon, so you'll be able to have a word with him.'

'That's good,' said Tony Blake. 'I've all but finished checking round.'

Holly went back up to the others. She told them about catching Jamie listening in on the crossed line.

'You've got to admit,' said Tracy, 'it is kind of intriguing, isn't it?

'I hope you're not suggesting we should try hunting for it,' said Belinda. 'I've been on enough wild goose chases for my liking. Besides it wouldn't be very fair.'

'Oh, I know,' agreed Tracy. 'But couldn't we just take a look at the information we've got? You know, just to see if we *could* figure it out if we wanted to? There's no harm in that, surely?'

'I suppose not,' said Holly. She knew she shouldn't, but the more they talked about it, the more intrigued she became. And after all, Jamie need never know. Holly smiled. 'It might be fun. I'll tell you what, I'll go and get Jamie's scribbles and we'll see what we can work out from what he overheard.'

On her way downstairs, Holly was surprised to see Tony Blake through the open front door, heading towards his van.

That's odd, she said to herself. *I thought he wanted to talk to Dad.* As she watched from the hallway, Tony Blake climbed into his van and drove rapidly away.

She shrugged, assuming that something important had come up that had to be dealt with.

She went into the kitchen and lifted the lid of the bin. The scrunched-up piece of paper should have been at the top. But it wasn't there.

'Jamie!' cried Holly. 'The little monster!'

She ran up to his room.

There was no sign of him. He had crept out of the house without finishing his chores. Despite everything she had said to him, it looked as if he intended searching for the amulet after all.

TITLES AVAILABLE IN THE MYSTERY CLUB SERIES

All these books are available at your local bookshop or newsagent or can be ordered direct from the publisher. Just tick the titles you want and fill in the form below.

Prices and availability subject to change without notice.

HODDER AND STOUGHTON PAPERBACKS, PO Box 11, Falmouth, Cornwall.

Please send cheque or postal order for the value of the book, and add the following for postage and packing.
UK including BFPO – £1.00 for one book, plus 50p for the second book, and 30p for each additional book ordered up to a £3.00 maximum.
OVERSEAS INCLUDING EIRE – £2.00 for the first book, plus £1.00 for the second book, and 50p for each additional book ordered.
OR Please debit this amount from my Access/Visa Card (delete as appropriate).

Card Number

Amount £...

Expiry Date...

Signed ....

Name...

Address...

....